MW01017590

In the Twilight

and

More Stories for Young Men

The stories in this book were complied from two different series, Sunshine Stories and Sabbath Readings. These stories were originally gathered from church papers in the 1870's, Methodists, Lutheran, Presbyterian, etc. We have found the stories to be truly "a breath of fresh air" in literature for children and youth. May they receive a warm welcome in your home is our prayer.

The Publishers.

A. B. Publishing
3039 S. Bagley
Ithaca, Mi 48847

Contents

In the Twilight 7
A German Story 14
The Noble Revenge...17
My Mother's Voice...19
God Seen in All His Works 22
Obedience Or Sacrifice 25
"Father! Don't Go!"..30
Honesty 33
Conversation about Tobacco...............................35
A Hermit and His Pitcher 39
Three Calico Gowns 41
The Interrupted Sermon 50
Child at Prayer 56
Not Good. Not Bad. 58
The Hermit and the Traveler 61
Peter Crisp's Spectacles.................................... 65
Stick to Your Business 71
"That's Thee, Jem!".. 74
The Widow's Mite.. 77
The King and the Farmer 86
Worth Better than Show.................................... 88
A Legacy 91
Farmer Penniman's Dream................................. 96
The Way of Escape 114
Quarrelsome Neighbor 130
A Change of Place 139
The Blighted Life 144
Not Myself... 152

In the Twilight

In a cheerful sitting room in one of our Western homes, at the close of the day, a happy group of friends were gathered. A young man who had been perusing a paper by the window in the twilight came forward and joined the happy circle around the table. From his brown cheek and full chest we arrive at the conclusion that he is a young farmer of about eighteen years of age. As he took his seat, a cheerful voice greeted him with, "Well, Emerson, what's the news?"

"Nothing in particular, Uncle Ben," replied Emerson, "but I was reading an offer for premiums to the young people for their best compositions."

"Ah! Are you going to try?"

"I! Why, Uncle, do you suppose a young farmer of limited education can produce anything worth reading?"

"Well, I will answer your question if you will tell me what your opinion is in regard to the editor's offers," said Uncle Ben.

"Well, Uncle," replies Emerson after a few moments consideration, "it seems to me that it is intended to draw forth and develop those powers of the mind which place the mental above physical life and which serve to educate and refine the young. And I think this offer is designed to prove that the efforts made by the writers to win the prize would result in as great benefit to those who were unsuccessful as to those who gain the prizes."

"Exactly," said Uncle Ben. "The influence is thrown in the right direction. Habits that are acquired in boyhood are sure to be found in the man, as my own experience has taught me too well. In fact, children," continued Uncle Ben, "I have a mind to tell you a story of my early life."

"Do, Uncle Ben, do," came from a chorus of voices.

As Uncle Ben announced his intention of telling a story, all eyes were turned upon him. Mother laid aside her book and her spectacles, for she had been reading before the twilight deepened. Father leaned back in his easy chair and seemed to listen with as deep interest as we children did. He knew how well Uncle Ben's mind was stored with rich incidents. While Uncle spoke, we thought he looked very sad. Placing his feet upon a footstool, he presently proceeded as follows,   "Many years ago, after my college education was completed, I had a strong desire for a situation on one of the railways that was then being laid through the United States. Through the influence of my friends, I received a position as fireman on one of the leading roads. I soon won the esteem and goodwill of all the officers and employees on the road. As time passed on, the superintendent and myself became deeply attached. We were about the same age. There was nothing I would not do for Frank Benway. I realized the duties of my position and determined to discharge them honorably.

"But, children, I was led away—led down, down, where so many have gone before and since! I was induced by the thoughtless associates to drink. What came next? I drank again, and again. One evening I had drank more than usual, when Frank Benway came in. I did not see him until he touched me on the arm.

"'Ben,' said he, 'come away. For my sake, come.'

"He took my arm and led me out into the cool night air. When he spoke again, it was in a pleading sorrowful tone.

"'Ben, for the sake of your mother, for the friendship between us, never drink again. Good night, my dear friend.'

"I went to my lodgings with a dizzy head and heavy heart. I knew that Frank ought to turn me away from my situation, but he was too noble, had too much confidence in me, even yet, to do that.

"When I awoke the next morning, I felt the strong thirst for liquor on me again. I found a flask in one of my pockets, filled with brandy, which I had procured the night previous. I had started down the hill and could not resist the temptation to drink *just once more!* The superintendent had gone down the road on an express train, early that morning, as there were some repairs being made, part way down the line, which he wished to superintend, personally.

"Our train started in about an hour after the express. The engineer of our train had been detained at the other end of the road on account of sickness. I was alone on the engine, but the conductor had perfect confidence in my ability. Alas! He would have mistrusted me had he known that I was at that very moment, mad and dazed with liquor! I had never drank enough to become intoxicated before, and no one on the train suspected I had formed the fatal habit. Still I drank until I became so helpless that I could not stand.

"I fell against the tender soon after we got under headway and cut a severe gash in my forehead. I attempted to rise but could not. My senses were clear, however, and I knew all that was passing, with horrible reality. I had fallen in such a position that I could see out on one side, between the tender and the engine. On, on we swept at lightning speed, with no hand to stop or regulate it. We had just passed the point where they were making the repairs I spoke of, and as we swept around a little bend in the road, I saw Frank Benway, a few steps ahead of us walking swiftly up the track. The moment I saw him, he stepped upon a bit of stone which lay there, purposely, it seemed to me, to lure him to death; and slipping, his foot was caught between the ground and the rail. Poor Frank struggled to rise, but could not. On we rushed, and Frank's efforts were all in vain. Oh, children! The bitterest part of my story is the knowledge that had I not been intoxicated I could have reversed the steam, probably in time to have saved his life!

"There I lay too intoxicated to move! As we came nearer, Frank saw me, for he had fallen across the track on the side where I lay on the locomotive, and he held out both hands imploringly to me, as if to say 'Help me, Ben, help me!' In another moment I was so near I could look into his eyes, and the next they were closed forever. A brakesman who saw Frank when we passed over him, now rushed to the engine and finding me lying disgracefully stupid, divined it all. He stopped the train. Frank's remains were gathered up, and I was taken to my home a raving maniac. None on the train save this man suspected I had been drunk. He kept my secret—why I never knew. Perhaps he felt I was punished enough. I was ill with brain fever a long time.

"After I recovered, I *never* tasted another drop of liquor.   It seemed as if I were more than a murderer. Afterward, when I went on the road again, I was a changed man. I gradually worked myself up until I became president of the road.

"I have seen my youth's companions pass away, one by one, and I know I shall join them ere long.   Yet I would say a few words to you, my dear ones, before I go. When you pass out from your parents' care, there will be many temptations to allure you. Then, I trust, you will bear in mind the evening when you all sat 'round Uncle Ben's knee and heard his sad story, told *in the twilight* of his life."

Remember

O youth! In your promise, your faith and your pride,
Remember, remember the strength of the tide.

It sweeps down the current the good and the brave,
And has in its bosom a gulf and a grave.

The wine cup may sparkle with beams of the sun,
Remember, remember from whence it is won.

It comes with its pleasures that change into pains;
It comes with its promise but never remains.

How many have traveled with light heart and free,
Remember, remember the way to the sea!

But free heart and light heart have vanished away,
And doubt and the darkness have shadowed the day.

The spell of the tempter is subtle, yet strong!
Remember, remember it binds to the wrong.

Then nothing can save you! Nothing recall
The hopes that will vanish away at your fall.

The loved you may cherish—the flowers of the heart,
Remember, remember with all, all depart.

The blossoms of springtime, the roses of May,

Like vapors of morning, will vanish away.

The promise of manhood, pride, honor and fame,
Remember, remember will change into shame.

And on life's record this epitaph stand:
"He died by the poison that curses the land."

O brother! My brother! To you I appeal!
Remember, remember, you win woe or weal.

Though tide is against you, though current is swift,
The Pharos of safety shines over the drift.

Hard out o'er the waters a beckoning hand,
Remember, remember, points out the sure land.

'Tis the temperance signal that floats in the air,
O brother! My brother! True safety is there!

A German Story

During a walk that I once had with the clergyman of Landsdroff and his wife, they told me of a sudden death which had lately taken place in the village.

"It is awful," I said, "what a thread life hangs upon!"

"That was really the case with one of my family in times past," said the clergyman's good wife. "Her life did hang by a thread."

"Tell me how it was," I said.

"It was that story," said the lady, "which caused the inscription you see to be placed over our doorway."

The inscription was as follows:

"If once we learn why God sends grief and woe,
How great His boundless love we then should know."

I read the lines, and then asked the minister's wife if she would kindly tell me the story.

She thus began, "About a hundred years ago, my mother's great aunt, the Countess Von Merits, was living with her two daughters in a castle in Germany.

"They were once invited to a wedding which was to take place by torchlight, according to the old German custom. They did not, accordingly, set out till it was beginning to get dusk. They had to pass on their way through a part of the Black Forest.

"Now it happened that Gertrude had a wreath of pearls given her, and she wore them on the evening of the wedding. But it chanced as they entered the forest, that a branch of black thorn caught her hair, and before it could be disentangled, the thread broke, and the small seed pearls were scattered far and wide.

"The servants and ladies busied themselves alike in picking up the scattered pearls, when suddenly a woodcutter came running from the forest and went up quite out of breath to the Countess.

"'Pray go no further, ladies!' he exclaimed. 'When I was cleaving wood just now, I heard two robbers planning how they might waylay your party, rob you, and kill your servants if they made any resistance. I had the greatest difficulty in getting to you in time. If you had not been later than you expected, you would most certainly have fallen into the hands of these robbers.'

"Of course no more was said about going on to the wedding, and the horses' heads were directly turned homeward. On arriving safely at her castle, the good mother thanked God, who had preserved her and those with her. Nor did she forget to reward the woodcutter, who had warned her in time of her danger. And there were two lessons which she tried to draw for her children from the history of that evening. First, that our life always hangs on as weak a thread as that which held Gertrude's pearls and that therefore God only keeps us alive; and, secondly, that all troubles and disappointments are as much sent for our good as the delay in getting to the wedding, which saved the family from the robbers.

"From this time," continued the clergyman's wife, "the lines you read over our door became the motto of the Countess and her family. And when I married, and my husband had the parsonage repaired, he inscribed, over the entrance:

"'If we learn why God sends grief and woe,
How great His boundless love we then should know.'"

The Noble Revenge

The coffin was a plain one—a poor, miserable, pine coffin. No flowers on its top, no lining of rose-white satin for the pale brow, no smooth ribbons about the coarse shroud. The brown hair was laid decently back, but there was no crimped cap with its neat tie beneath he chin. The sufferer from cruel poverty smiled in her sleep.

"I want to see my mother," sobbed a poor child, as the city undertaker screwed down the top.

"You can't—get out of the way, boy! Why don't somebody take the brat?"

"Only let me see her one minute," cried the hapless, homeless orphan, clutching the side of the charity box, and as he gazed into that rough face, anguish tears streamed rapidly down the cheek on which no childish bloom ever lingered. Oh, it was pitiful to hear him cry, "Only once, let me see my mother only once!"

Quickly and brutally the hard-hearted monster struck the boy away, so that he reeled with the blow. For a moment the boy stood panting with grief and rage; his blue eye distended, his lips sprang apart, a fire glittering through his tears, as he raised his puny arm, and with a most unchildish accent screamed, "When I'm a man, I'll *kill* you for that!"

There was a coffin and a heap of earth between the mother and the poor, forsaken child, and a monument stronger than granite built in the boy's heart to the memory of a heartless deed.

The courthouse was crowded to suffocation.

"Does any one appear as this man's counsel?" asked the judge.

There was a silence when he finished, until, with lips pressed together and a look of strange intelligence blended with haughty reserve upon his handsome features, a young man stepped forward with a firm tread and kindling eye, to plead for the erring and the friendless. He was a stranger, but from his first sentence there was silence.

The splendor of his genius entranced and convinced. The man who could not find a friend was acquitted.

"May God bless you, sir, I cannot."

"I want no thanks," replied the stranger, with icy coldness.

"I—I believe you are unknown to me."

"Man! I will refresh your memory. Twenty years ago you struck a brokenhearted boy away from his mother's poor coffin. *I* was that poor, miserable boy."

The man turned livid.

"Have you rescued me, then, to take my life?"

"No, I have a sweeter revenge; I have saved the life of a man whose brutal deed has rankled in my breast for twenty years. Go! And remember the tears of a friendless child."

The man bowed his head in shame and went out from the presence of a magnanimity as grand to him as incomprehensible, and the noble young lawyer felt God's smile in his soul.

My Mother's Voice

A friend told me not long ago a beautiful story about kind words. A good lady passed a drinking saloon just as the keeper was thrusting a young man into the street. He was quite young and very pale, but his haggard face and wild eyes told that he was far gone in the road to ruin, and with an oath he brandished his clenched fists, threatening to be revenged on the man who had ill-used him. This young man was so excited and blinded with passion, that he did not see the lady who stood very near to him, until she laid her hand on his arm, and spoke in her gentle, loving voice, asking him what was the matter.

At the first kind word he started as if a heavy blow had struck him, and turned quickly 'round paler than before, trembling from head to foot. He surveyed the lady for a moment, and then with a sigh of relief he said, "I thought that was my mother's voice; it sounded strangely like! But her voice has been hushed in death these many years."

"You had a mother then, and she loved you," said she.

With that sudden revulsion of feeling which often comes to people of fine nervous temperaments, the young man burst into tears and sobbed out, "Oh yes, I had an angel mother and she loved her boy! But since she died all the world has been against me, and I am lost to honor, lost to decency, and lost forever!"

"No, not lost forever, for God is merciful, and His pitying love can reach the chief of sinners," said the lady in her soft, sweet voice. The timely words swept the hidden chords of feeling which had long been untouched in the young man's heart, thrilling it with magic power, and wakening a host of tender emotions, which had been buried deep beneath the rubbish of sin and crime.

More gentle words the lady spoke, and when she passed on her way the young man followed her. He marked the house she entered and wrote the name which was on the silver doorplate in his memorandum book. Then he went slowly away with a very earnest look on his pale face and a deeper and more earnest feeling in his heart.

Years glided by, and the gentle lady had quite forgotten the incident we have related, when one day a stranger sent up his card and desired to speak with her.

Wondering who it could be, she went down to the parlor where she found a noble-looking, well-dressed man, who rose deferentially to meet her. Holding out his hand, he said, "Pardon me, madam, for this intrusion, but I have come many miles to thank you for the great service you rendered me a few years ago," said he, in a trembling voice.

The lady was puzzled and asked for an explanation, as she did not remember ever having seen the gentleman before.

"I have changed much," said the man, "that you have quite forgotten me; but though I only saw your face once, I am sure I should have recognized it anywhere. And your voice, too, is so like my mother's."

These last words made the lady remember the young man she had kindly spoken to in front of the drinking saloon so long before and the tears flowed freely—both wept. After the first gush of emotion had subsided, the gentleman told the lady how those few gentle words had been instrumental in saving him and making him what he was then.

"The earnest expression of 'No, not lost forever,' followed me wherever I went," said he, "and it always seemed that it was the voice of my mother speaking to me from the tomb. I repented of my many transgressions and resolved to live in Jesus as my mother would have been pleased to have had me; and by the mercy and grace of God I have been enabled to resist temptation and keep my good resolutions."

"I never dreamed there was such power in a few kind words before," exclaimed the lady, "and surely, ever after this, I shall take more pains to speak them to all the sad and suffering ones I meet in the walks of life."

God Seen in All His Works

In that beautiful part of Germany which borders on the Rhine, there is a noble castle, as you travel on the west bank of the river, which you may see lifting its ancient towers on the opposite side, above the grove of trees about as old as itself. About forty years ago, there lived in that castle a noble gentleman, Baron Philippie. He had only one son, who was not only a companion and a comfort to his father, but a blessing to all who lived on his father's estate. It happened, on a certain occasion, that, this young man being from home, there came a French gentleman to the castle, who began to talk of his heavenly Father in terms that chilled the old Baron's blood, who reproved him, saying, "Are you not afraid of offending God?" The gentleman replied that he was not, for he had never seen Him.

The Baron did not notice the answer, but the next morning he took his visitor about the castle grounds and, among other objects, showed him a very beautiful picture that hung on the wall. The gentleman admired it very much and remarked that whoever drew that picture, knew how to use the pencil.

"My son drew that picture," said the Baron.

"Then your son is a clever man," replied the gentleman.

The Baron then went with his visitor into the garden and showed him beautiful flowers and the plantations of forest trees.

"Who had the ordering of this garden?" asked the gentleman.

"My son," replied the Baron, "he knows every plant here, from the cedar of Lebanon to the hyssop on the wall."

"Indeed," replied the gentleman, "I shall think very highly of him soon."

The Baron then took him into the village and showed him a small, neat cottage, where his son had established a school, and where he caused all young people who had lost their parents to be received and nourished at his expense. The children in the house looked so innocent and so happy that the gentleman was very much pleased, and when he returned to the castle, he said to the Baron, "What a happy man you are to have so good a son?"

"How do you know that I have so good a son?"

"Because I have seen his works, and I know that he must be good and clever if he has done all that you have showed me."

"And you have not seen him?"

"No, but I know him very well for I judge of him by his works."

"True," replied the Baron, "and in this way I judge the character of our heavenly Father. I know by His works that He is a being of infinite wisdom, power, and goodness."

The French gentleman felt the force of reproof and was careful not to offend the good old Baron any more by his remarks.

Creation

All things bright and beautiful,
   All creatures great and small,
All things wise and wonderful,
   The Lord God made them all.

He gave us eyes to see them,
   And lips, that we might tell
How great is God Almighty,
   Who has made all things well.

Obedience Or Sacrifice?

"I wish I had lived in those times!" exclaimed Henry Sharp, a rather enthusiastic boy, as he finished reading the account of the death of Latimer and Ridley.

"Why?" inquired Mr. Severn, his tutor.

"Because I should like to have been a martyr," replied Henry slowly; "it seems such a glorious thing to die for what you believe to be right."

The opinion did not seem to be in the least shared by his schoolfellows, who showed their astonishment and dissent by various gestures. Some were ready to laugh and looked towards the master, with faces expressive of their ideas of their own superior wisdom, and anticipating the rebuke that was to fall upon their comrade.

But Mr. Severn was not a man to judge things hastily or to pronounce a remark silly, and to leave it without trying to explain the matter, so he said quietly, "Do you really think so, Henry? Do you believe that you would have the courage and firmness to submit to the severe and often lingering agonies which those persecuted men endured?"

"Of course I can't be sure that I should, sir," replied Henry, "but it seems to me that the thought of gaining heaven must be enough to sustain any one in ever so much pain."

"I can sympathize with your feelings," continued Mr. Severn, "for I remember as a boy to have had the same idea; but as I grew older and able to understand the state of my own heart better, I came to the conclusion that I was deceiving myself.

"I found out, in examining myself, that while thus longing for martyrdom as a means of gaining heaven, I was unconsciously looking upon that pain and suffering as more easy to bear than the yoke which Christ has laid upon us. Or to express myself more simply, I mean that I was really thinking I would rather submit to a cruel death than struggle daily and hourly to live as Jesus would have me live. While fancying I was wishing to give the strongest proof of my love to God, I was really shrinking from the service He had appointed me and trying to find out an easier way for myself.

"I cannot of course tell what you feel," continued Mr. Severn; "I only give you my own experience to guide you, but I must add further caution—martyrdom is not a certain means of entering heaven."

"Not certain!" exclaimed several of his hearers, and Henry looked particularly astonished.

"I admit," answered Mr. Severn, "that it is difficult to imagine a man willing to die for his religion, who has not a firm and saving faith in his Saviour; but that it may be the case, we have St. Paul's testimony—'Though I give my body to be burned and have not charity, it profiteth me nothing.'

"Many have tried to find out paths that please them better than God's narrow way. You remember the history of Naaman the Syrian. He went to Elisha to be cured of his leprosy and willing, as subsequent events proved, to do a great deal to get cured of his fearful and loathsome malady. But when the prophet sent out the message to him to go and dip seven times in the river Jordan, the very simplicity of the means to be employed offended him. If he had been told to undertake some weary pilgrimage, to go through some painful sufferings, no doubt he would have submitted cheerfully; but to wash in that river Jordan! His pride rebelled against it. Nay, even if he must be cured by washing, why not let it be the mightier streams of his own and, Abana and Pharpar, rivers of Damascus! Thus he argued—anything rather than what God's prophet appointed. And we are very much like Naaman. Sin is like leprosy, and when we ask to be cured of it, we are told that there is but one means—to wash in the fountain that is opened for all sin and for all uncleanness, to rely for cleansing upon the Lamb of God, who taketh away the sin of the world. Human pride revolts against this and would prefer a salvation which left man to 'do some great thing' for himself and did not merely place him in the purifying stream humbly and confidingly like a little child.

"We must not deceive ourselves but try and forget such fancies for doing some great thing and endeavor instead to do the everyday duties that are before us. So many more are called upon to perform such deeds, than to do great things, that I believe they are fully as pleasing in the sight of God, when done from a simple desire to His glory. We do His will in striving to perform our daily duties, however trivial and simple, as He would have them done; and in believing that, let them be what they will, it is noble work, because it is what He has given us to do. In the Bible how many instances we have of those who have employed their talents well, receiving more—of men called to greater honors or more extensive labor when they were simply employed in attending to their everyday concerns.

"A shepherd guarding his father-in-law's flock upon Mount Horeb—a voice comes to him and he is called to confront a powerful kin—to free, by signs and wonders, an enslaved people from his unwillingly relaxed grasp—to become the leader and lawgiver of this rescued nation, and to be a favored servant of God.

"Another youth, also employed in keeping sheep—the prophet sent to his father's house sees all his brothers, but does not find among them the chosen of the Lord. This youngest is then sent for from his humble occupation, and upon his head is poured the anointing oil and into his heart the sanctifying grace, which gains for him that glorious title, 'The man after God's own heart.'

"Another man plowing with twelve yoke of oxen—Israel's great prophet passes by and casts his mantle upon him, calling him to be his successor; yes, even to receive a double portion of the spirit which rested upon him, and he had stood fearless and alone on the side of God among the multitudes of Baal's prophets and the prophets of the groves.

"Where was Matthew when Jesus called him? At the receipt of custom. Where were Peter, James, and John? At their simple craft of fishing. Was not Gideon threshing wheat when called to be a judge of Israel? But I need not repeat any more examples; those I have quoted are sufficient to point out what I mean."

"I suppose my wish was a very foolish one," said Henry, "and I have been deceiving myself as you suspected. I have not looked at things in the light you represent them. The view you have would make us more contented with our lot, however humble. It certainly would cause us to feel more interest in our daily duties to think that they are part of God's work upon earth."

"It does indeed," answered Mr. Severn, "and to omit evident duties in order to select those we fancy would be better, is just as strange a way of showing our obedience as if you, when desired by me to prepare a page of Plato, were to bring up to the class a page of Sophocles instead. You might think it more difficult and greater merit, but it would not be what I had given you to do. The continual sense of our being about God's work, and of His eye seeing us, gives importance and worth to all we have to do."

Are there not many who like Henry feel that it would be a glorious thing to make some great sacrifice, who, perhaps, might find it very difficult to yield their will in very trivial matters or to submit to the discipline of parents and teachers, forgetting that "to obey is better than sacrifice or to hearken than the fat of rams"?

"Father! Don't Go."

That there is a sphere of influence possessed by everyone, not even excepting the child, was affectingly illustrated in the following incident.

"Some years ago," said the late Benjamin Rotch in one of his telling speeches, "I was addressing a public meeting in the neighborhood of Aylesbury, and in the course of my remarks I endeavored to enforce individual duty and the right exercise of individual influence. There sat, on the front form, a fine-looking but weather-beaten railway laborer, who paid very earnest attention to me. He had, sitting on his knee, a little girl about five years old. By the way of refuting the common excuse for indolence, 'I have no influence,' I remarked that the little girl sitting on the working man's knee in front of me, even she, had influence. The man, as if acting under some magic spell, jumped on his feet, put the child on the floor, and then striking his hand against his thigh exclaimed, 'That's true!'

"This singular interruption somewhat disconcerted me. The man, evidently embarrassed at what he had done, took his seat, reinstated his little girl on his knee, and again drank in the truths delivered to the meeting. As I was leaving the room this man was waiting at the door. I said to him, 'Now, my good man, tell me what induced you to conduct yourself in the way you did?'

"'Sometime ago,' said he, 'I was employed on the railway and was in the habit of going every night to a beer shop, from which I seldom returned sober. I had,' said he, with a big tear glistening in his eye, 'at that time a daughter of nineteen years of age; she was a dutiful child, with a warm and affectionate heart. She used to come after me to the beer shop, but she would never go inside, though I sometimes pressed her to do so. She would wait outside the door, in the cold and wet, until I came out that she might conduct me home. She was afraid, if left to myself, I might fall into some pit or down some precipice, and lose my life. By this conduct, poor thing, she caught a severe cold. It turned to consumption and she died.

"'I felt her death very much, though I still went to the beer shop; but somehow or other I never, after her death, liked to go that way alone, especially in the night. For the sake of company, I used to take with me the little girl whom you saw sitting on my knee tonight.

"'But one night,' he continued, 'I was walking along with the little girl, she holding onto my coat, and when we got very near the beer shop there was a great noise within, and my little girl shrank back and said, *"Father, don't go!"* Vexed with her I took her up in my arms and proceeded, but just as I was entering the beer-house door, I felt a scalding tear fall from her eyes. It went to my heart. I turned my back upon the public house. This was twelve months ago, and I have never tasted drink since. I could not help getting up and doing as I did; but I hope, sir, you will forgive me.'"

A father bore upon his arm
    A girl of tender years;
She shiver'd sadly with the cold,
    Her eyes were full of tears.

I paused to see why she would weep—
    A girl so young and fair—
And why her father wore a look
    Of horror and despair.

I did not need to tarry long
    Her tears to understand,
For on a gin-shop's half-shut door
    The father laid his hand.

Loud was the wintry wind without,
    Loud was the noise within;
But o'er them all I heard her words,
    "Oh! Father, don't go in!"

He turned him sternly from the door
    And strode along the street,
Thanking his young deliverer
    With words and kisses sweet.

Strong were the few and gentle words
    The little girl did speak;
But stronger far the silent tear
    That trickled down her cheek!

Honesty

Honesty is the outspoken truth, revealing the real character. The term honesty signifies justice and uprightness. A man is honest because it is his policy to deal honorable with all with whom he may have intercourse. When he sells you an article he demands an equivalent. The sharper covets more; he fills his purse at others' expense and generally gets the best side of the bargain.

Honesty in all things is a virtue few attain. Many conceal their true character under a cloak of deception. We are dishonest in a great many ways—in language, deed and action. Our lives are made up of little things; it is in these little things that we are the most dishonorable—more so, perhaps, than in larger deeds. Honesty is the best business qualification any young man can possess. Starting in life with determination to lead an honorable career begins a foundation at once secure, like a cornerstone upon which your future prosperity rests. Honesty believes in quick sales and small profits—in the one-price system. Honesty is not lavish in his statements but represents his goods as they are—their merits and defects—and uses no trap-like device to swindle the unwary.

The most notable example of true honesty was George Washington. Always methodical and equal to his promises, he gained a worldwide reputation as a trustworthy man. The adage, "A wrong confessed is half redressed," is a splendid one. Dishonesty may prosper for a while, but honesty is the most successful in the long run. Men most prosperous in all the thoroughfares of enterprise owe their good fortune to judicious dealing and uprightness in business.

The great need of the day is more honest men. We see at the present time crime, extensive defalcation and bartering for gold. Honesty ensures a clear conscience; it ensures peace of mind; it promotes confidence in each other; and above all it is the noblest of virtues.

Conversation about Tobacco

"Mother, how much tobacco does it take to make a sermon?"

"What do you mean, my son?"

"Why, I mean, how much tobacco does father chew, and how many cigars does he smoke while he is making a sermon?"

"Well, the tobacco and the cigars don't make the sermon, do they?"

"I don't know, but they do help along, at any rate, for I heard father tell Mr. Morris, the minister who preached for him last Sunday, that he could never write well without a good cigar. So I thought the tobacco makes the sermons, or the best part of them."

"My son, I am shocked to hear you talk so!"

"Well, Mother, I was only telling what Father said, and what it made me think. He said a prime cigar was a great solace (whatever that is); and he said besides it drove away the blues—put him into a happy frame of mind, and stimulated his brain, so he could work better. I've been thinking if I had something to stimulate my brain I could study better; and the next time I have one of those knotty questions in arithmetic to work out, I will get a cigar and see if it won't help me along. You know you often tell me if I follow my father's example I will not go very far astray, and now I would like a few cigars to make my brain work well so that I can stand at the head of my class."

"I hope I shall never see my son with a cigar in his mouth; it would be the first step to ruin."

"You don't think father is ruined, do you? And he has taken a good many steps since he took the first cigar."

"I think, my son, your father would be better without cigars or tobacco in any shape, but he formed the habit when he was young, and now it is hard to break it off."

"But Father says, 'We are to blame for forming habits, and it is a sin to continue them.' I heard him say that in the pulpit not long ago. There is old Tom Jenkins who drinks hard. I suppose he would find it rather hard to leave off drinking whiskey. But Father says, 'It is no excuse for a man, when he gets drunk, to say he is in the habit of getting drunk.' He says, 'People should exercise resolution and moral courage to break off bad habits.'"

"But, my son, smoking tobacco is not quite like drinking whiskey and getting drunk."

"No, I know that Mother; but I was going to say that if smoking was a bad habit, Father would have given it up long ago. If he could write as well and do as much good without using tobacco, he would not spend so much for it. When I want to buy a little candy or a bit of spruce gum, father tells me that I had better practice the grace of self-denial and save money for the missionary box. I heard Deacon Tomkins say his cigars cost him three hundred dollars a year for he uses none but the very best, and they are all imported. He told father so the other day, when they were smoking together in the study after dinner, and I was trying to get my arithmetic lesson. Now, Mother, do you think my father, and the deacon, and a whole host of ministers and elders, and temperance lecturers, and lots of good people would spend so much money to keep themselves in bad habits?   Why, just the sum that Deacon Tomkins spends on cigars would support a missionary in the West for a whole year.   Please, Mother, give me some money to get some cigars."

"My son, you may talk the matter over with your father.   Ask him if he thinks it will improve your habits and your health to smoke.   I think he will tell you that it will only do you harm."

Tobacco

What gives my breath an awful smell,
And hinders me from feeling well?
One single word the tale will tell!
     Tobacco.

What paints my skin a dirty brown,
What keeps my manly spirits down?
What turns a *man* into a clown?
     Tobacco.

What keeps me spitting all day
On fence and wall, till people say,
"I guess he'll spit his life away"?
     Tobacco.

I'll then no more my health abuse,
Nor chew this weed nor spit its juice;
I give my pledge to *never* use
     Tobacco.

I tell you friends, I will be free!
My passions' *slave* no more I'll be;
And in my mouth no man shall see
     Tobacco.

Now will my health return again,
I will be free from ache and pain,
For I have quit the dirty bane,
     Tobacco.

A Hermit and His Pitcher

He who bids adieu to the world, and retires into the wilderness does not for that reason become a saint; for so long as the inclination to evil dwells in the heart, temptation from without is easily found and sin is committed.

Experience taught this to the man of whom an old story gives account. This man was by nature prone to sudden bursts of passion, but, instead of seeking the cause of this fault in himself, he cast the blame upon the man who excited him to anger, and thought, "If this is so, the world is an injury to me, and it is better that I should leave it rather than lose my soul."

He withdrew, therefore, into the wilderness, and built himself a hut in the midst of a wood, close by a spring. The bread that he ate was brought daily to him by a boy, who had been directed to place it upon a rock at a distance from the hut.

And thus all went well for several days, and he thought that he had become the most mild and even-tempered man in the world.

One day, he went as usual with his pitcher to the spring and placed it so that the water might run into it. But as the ground was stony and uneven, the pitcher fell over. He placed it upright again and more carefully than before, but it was overturned a second time. Then he angrily seized the vessel and dashed it violently upon the ground so that it broke in pieces.

He now remarked that his old anger had broken forth again, and he thought, "If that is the case, the wilderness can in no way profit me, and it is better that I try to save my soul in the world, by avoiding that which is evil and practicing that which is good." And he returned into the world.

Observe—there are evil inclinations which may be conquered by avoiding the occasions which call them forth, and there are others which must be vanquished by resistance. But to perform either, we need not fly from the world but from ourselves only.

Three Calico Gowns

Judge Clinton would insist upon living in a little brown, old-fashioned house without carpets upon the floors, and, what was more vexations, he would not allow a sofa or lounge or rocking chair inside the four brown walls. As he had an idea that the whole country was going to rack and ruin because the men wore broadcloth, and the women wore silks, he declared he would wear homespun as long as he lived and his women folks should be restricted to calico.

As we have nothing to do with Mrs. Judge Clinton, we shall not allude to the hearty vexation with which she carried out the judge's whimsical notions. But she could do nothing wiser than to swallow and, womanlike, pretend to believe, with her husband, that they could reform the world by making themselves conspicuously mean and uncomfortable.

Judge Clinton was still in indigo-colored homespun and Mrs. Judge Clinton in nine-penny calico when Miss Clara Clinton, having reached the age of eighteen and having a will of her own (which her mother was careful to tell everybody the child inherited from her father), announced her desire and determination to go to a boarding school.

The judge himself had been a poor boy, educated through his own exertions. He was a proof of his humble birth and the difficulties he had overcome at Brundery. He had read Virgil by the aid of a penny candle, and solved the problems of Euclid by moonlight. He respected but one desire in the world, and that was a thirst for knowledge. So when Miss Clara protested that she must, and could, and would go to a boarding school, Judge Clinton cheerfully acquiesced and expressed himself ready to "cash over."

No sooner was this interesting subject broached, however, than, to Miss Clara's surprise, her father selected the most expensive, thorough, and aristocratic institution in the country, paid the yearly expenses in advance, and sent her at once to complete her education, with twenty-five cents for spending money and three calico gowns for her wardrobe.

It was bad enough, Miss Clara said, sobbing all the while, to be obliged to dress in calico; but to have three calico gowns all alike, from the self-same piece, so that her companions would think she had but one—that was "the hardest to bear of all."

But the old judge was incorrigible. He had saved two shillings and sixpence by having them all alike, and he was satisfied, if his daughter was not.

It was a bright, clear May morning when Miss Clara bid adieu to the ugly brown homestead, to her mother, who wiped her tears on her calico apron, and to the sheep that bore the fleeces from which her father's homespun was made. She loved everything about the dun dwelling now that she looked upon it from the coach window. But soon the novelty of her condition overcame her grief, and she forgot all the petty vexations in the new scenes and strange people around her.

Very weary and travel-soiled, she alighted at the end of her journey and was shown into the reception room,

where were seated several stylish young ladies, evidently
newly arrived pupils like herself.

There was Miss June with her exquisitely fitting
gray traveling dress, who glanced her over with a quizzical
look in her dark eyes. Miss Clara felt sure that the peculiar
smiles that lingered upon those sarcastic lips owed their
existence to the fact that she wore "calico."

Blushing to her very temples, poor Clara looked
away, only to encounter the gaze of Miss Gay, who,
reclining upon the sofa in the most faultless attire, seemed
absorbed in studying the pattern of the print.

Miss Gay and Miss June exchanged glances and
smiles. Tears welled up from Clara's full heart, but she was
too proud to wipe them away; one fell, then another, when a
soft voice said, "You are very tired, I am sure; so are we all,
but we shall be attended to soon."

Clara looked her thanks to the gentle speaker—a
girl very plainly dressed and of sweet, winsome
countenance, who, bringing a chair nearer, asked her some
trivial questions and related some amusing experiences of
her own in reaching the institution.

Clara felt more at ease, and, being naturally
vivacious and intelligent, soon made friends with the kind
stranger, who invited her to become her roommate.

The school term soon commenced, and there was
little time for Clara to think of her homely garments. But
when Sunday came round, and she took another calico dress
from her wardrobe, exactly like the one she had worn all the
week, her roommate said, "Miss Clinton, I beg your pardon,
but wouldn't something else do better today? The young
ladies usually dress a good deal here, especially the first

Sunday of appearing, and I am afraid you will not find it pleasant to be so plainly attired."

Clara blushed, but she was a brave-hearted girl and had the good sense to know that deception could avail nothing. So she said frankly, "The truth is, I have but three dresses in the world, and those are exactly alike!"

Miss Pleasant looked at her a moment as if she thought she must be quizzing, but, perceiving the blushes and confusion of her roommate, burst out laughing!

"Why, Clara! It is so comical! You must excuse me, dear, if I do laugh a little. How does it happen you dress so plainly?"

"Well, my father is very odd in some things, and it is his will that we dress in prints."

Miss Pleasant went to the closet and shaking out a plain but very presentable black silk, said, "Please wear this, dear Clara. Don't think but I shall love you just as well in calico, but many of the girls won't, and you are so sensitive you will be wounded. I can well do without this dress the whole term, and no one will know but it is yours."

Clara hesitated. She had always desired a silk dress. She had been thinking all the morning of the ridicule of her schoolmates. Should she accept this offered kindness? Or would it be better to wear her own clothes and appear as she really was?

She did not hesitate long, but putting her arms around Miss Pleasant's neck, kissed her with trembling lips, then said in a quiet way, "Thank you, thank you a thousand times. It does not seem best. My father would not approve it, nor do I. If you love me, that is enough."

Miss Pleasant patted Clara's cheek gently, murmuring, "You are right, Clara, and you are handsomer in your calico than the richest of them in all their silks and finery."

Nothing more was said. The two girls went down to the assembly room when the bell rang and found the people standing in groups, waiting the appearance of the assistant teacher to lead them to church.

"Look! Will you?" whispered Miss Gay to the young lady next to her, "If that girl isn't going to church in that calico dress."

Miss Pleasant frowned, but Clara smiled. She had conquered her pride that morning on her knees; she had resolved not to be made unhappy by what she could not help.

The assistant teacher entered the room with a rustle and a trail befitting her station. She looked the young ladies over with a sweeping glance and peremptorily ordered Miss Clara Clinton to her room.

Miss Pleasant whispered a word in that lady's ear; Miss Clara was recalled, and the procession fell into line. It was very vexatious that all the gentlemen those young ladies passed seemed to look only at the calico dress. It was so very odd to see a young lady going to church in print. From the dress they looked into the face—such a pretty face as it was, too, so bright—all thinking of the oddity of the attire and wondering who the young lady could be.

It was not long before Clara became known as the young lady in calico. Old Mr. Vennet, the wealthiest and most influential gentleman of the town, having had his attention directed to her peculiar dress, made the discovery that her father had been his dear and intimate friend in college. He also was self-made, and he and Judge Clinton had walked together in the thorny ways of poverty.

Mr. Vennet, at the first opportunity, sent a carriage to bring Miss Clara to dine with his family and told her many stories of which Judge Clinton was the hero. He was evidently very proud of his friend's pretty daughter.

Afterward, he from time to time sent bouquets from his rare exotics and such abundance of fruit, besides taking her to ride occasionally with his family, that the young ladies of the institute were almost in a state of envy. Finally, as if to drive the young ladies distraction, the Vennets gave a party to which the most influential and wealthiest families of the county were invited. Even the principal of the institute was overlooked.

As might be expected, Miss Clinton from that evening was quite a belle. No one could slight a young lady to whom the Vennets had been so attentive. Besides, there was something quite novel in having a beautiful young creature from the country who had a rich father and wore calico because she was not poor! The young ladies petted her because they had nothing to be jealous of; the old ladies patronized her as an example for their daughters; the young men respected her for her pretty ways, independence of character, and ready wit; and the old men put their thumbs into the arms of their vests and gravely announced that "she was quite the original and exemplary young lady, and they wished there were more like her." Indeed, the only trouble was that Judge Clinton's calico dresses didn't prove his daughter's ruin.

The long school session was to close with a public examination, upon which occasion all the young ladies were required to wear white with satin sashes and a rosette upon the left shoulder. The principal had an eye to effect, and she would admit nothing that disturbed harmony.

Miss Clinton's calico gown was vetoed at once. "It would do very well, perhaps, for Mr. Vennet's party, but it was not proper for an examination!" So Judge Clinton received a very polite note from the formidable lady, requesting him in frigid and unmistakable terms "to allow his daughter white mull."

If the principal had designed to make Judge Clinton the happiest of men, which she didn't, and to render it forever out of Miss Clara's power to wear white mull, she could not more effectually have accomplished her purpose than in writing him this note.

Judge Clinton, of Clintonville, declared that he was not the man to be dictated to by any woman—not he; and precisely because it would oblige her to have Clara dress in white, it would disoblige him to do so. His rather impolite reply was: "I sent my daughter to school to study books, not dress. If you wanted my daughter to wear white, you are at liberty to provide that garment for her. For my part I do not know what right teachers have to decide what color or goods their pupils should wear. If you are not willing my daughter should appear in print, you are at liberty to say so and I will remove her at once from the school."

The principal, as may be supposed, was as indignant as a principal could well be. But what would the Vennets say and the wealthy persons whom they would influence, if Miss Clara was banished for wearing a dress they had condescended to honor?

Besides, Clara was the best writer, the best singer and the best dialogue-maker of the whole school. She was necessary to the brilliancy of the anniversary.

The principal decided to adopt the judge's suggestion and provide the outfit at her own expense. But no sooner was this decided upon, than the judge wrote by express, protesting that his daughter *should not wear white at all*, and that he was coming in person to see that she did not violate his command.

The result of it was, the judge carried his point and Clara was the odd bird in the whole flock of white pigeons.

Among all the queens of the Swiss and mull, the rustic belle was observed of all observers. She was really the handsomest, merriest, and most sparkling creature in the room.

And what was sadly provoking to the principal, there sat Judge Clinton, in his suit of homespun, by the side of old Mr. Vennet, upon the platform, availing himself of every opportunity to tell the whole story connected with the calico garment, and turning the confused teacher to ridicule.

At last it came to the distribution of the prizes, and that for exemplary conduct and correct recitations was awarded to Miss Clara Clinton.

Judge Clinton did not make a speech on that occasion; it was because Mr. Vennet did. As the address was fully reported at the time of delivery, we will not report it here, but simply refer to that part of it which relates to our heroine.

"I am happy," said Mr. Vennet, "that this prize has fallen to the daughter of my friend, Judge Clinton, of Clintonville. She is a worthy daughter of a worthy sire. She may well be proud to have received this token of her teacher's approbation, for she has won it under peculiar and trying circumstances. Young ladies, do not forget that though you are beautiful when adorned, you are more attractive, more intellectual, more self-reliant while you remain satisfied with what Providence has placed at your disposal."

The Interrupted Sermon

One evening I was chatting with my friend, the minister, in his study. My attention was turned to a beautifully embroidered text, which was suspended on the wall. It was the passage in 1 Peter 1:24, 25 that reads as follows: "All flesh is as grass, and all the glory of man as the flower of grass. The grass withereth, and the flower thereof falleth away; but the word of the Lord endureth forever."

"What an exquisite piece of needlework this is!" I said. "It is quite wonderful."

"It is," he answered; "but more wonderful still were the remarkable leadings of God of which this picture is a remembrance."

"Really!" I rejoined. "And would it be indiscreet—"

"Oh, I shall be delighted to tell you the story," he interrupted kindly. "It takes me back some twenty-five years, when as yet I was a young preacher. I think that I am justified in saying that I tried to preach the gospel to the best of my knowledge, but I must add that my knowledge was sadly limited. I thought that, to be useful, I ought, above all things, to exercise myself in the rhetoric art and in the elegant forms of eloquence. Now, certainly nobody will assert that rhetoric and eloquence are arts which a preacher of the gospel should neglect. Robert Hall, for instance, was no less a preacher of truth because he clothed his thoughts in oratorical language; but I overdid the thing. As my vanity was well pleased when I saw numbers, especially of the higher and wealthier class, attracted to me by the beauties of my style and the power of my elocution, I selected those subjects which afforded more scope for display and devoted almost all my time during the week to my sermons, which, after having been carefully 'planned and polished,' were, word for word, committed to memory. The consequence was that the contents of my sermons became very poor and shallow; and the plain truths of the gospel, which speak of sin, of righteousness, and of judgment, if introduced at all, were all but buried under the artificial flowers of oratory.

"'My dear,' my good wife would sometimes say, 'I am afraid you are making more admirers of yourself than followers of Jesus.'

"'How so, my dear?' I would ask testily; 'didn't you like my sermon this morning?'

"'Well,' the answer would be, 'I cannot but say that you preached beautifully and that all you said was quite true so far as it went; but there are many other precious and important truths which you seldom or never preach about, and which yet we are greatly in need of.'

"And so she would often in her closet commit the matter to God, and pray Him to teach me to lead those who are dead in trespasses and sins to a living, loving, and life-giving Christ.

"It passed the Lord to hear that prayer of my excellent wife. One Sunday morning I preached as usual to a crowded congregation, chiefly composed of the principal inhabitants of the neighborhood. I was just then engaged in giving my audience a picturesque description of a sunset on the Sea of Galilee, when all on a sudden, owing to the close atmosphere, a little girl fell into a fainting fit. The disturbances which it created, though only short and comparatively insignificant, yet so much put me out that I became altogether confused. The rest of my sermon all at once vanished from my memory. I could not possibly recollect one word of it. In my perplexity I cried to God for help. While looking down on my Bible, which was lying open before me, my eye fell upon the text of Peter which you see yonder suspended on the wall. Yielding, as it were, to an instinctive impulse, I read it to my hearers and began preaching from it an improvised sermon just as it came up in my heart. And here, having lost my oratorical flower basket, I could not help laying bare the truths of God's Word in all their simplicity and startling reality. Connecting the text with my previous description, I compared the glory of man to the setting of the sun, which was never to rise again. I spoke of the utter vanity of everything human, of the certainty of the destruction of this world, and of our everlasting condemnation if we were to die in the midst of our sins. In a word, I 'shunned not to declare to them all the counsel of God,' proclaiming death and destruction as it is in Adam, and life and salvation as it is in Jesus.

"On walking home after service my wife almost wept for joy. Never in her life, she said, had she heard such a heart-searching sermon. But I was in an almost desponding mood of mind and quite ashamed of myself, 'for the people must have noticed my confusion,' I said, 'and what a gossip will it be all over the place that the minister broke down in the middle of his sermon! Surely,' I added, 'this was the worst sermon ever preached from a pulpit.'

"We had scarcely got home, however, when a lady desired to speak to me. The impression which her appearance made upon me was not very agreeable. She was gaudily dressed and carried a flourish of trinkets, lace, and finery about her which created a most unfavorable impression.

"'Sir,' she said, while her lip quivered, 'could you permit me to speak to you in confidence?'

"'Certainly, ma'am.'

"'I am a lost woman,' she said, while tears burst from her eyes, 'but you, sir, can perhaps tell me whether there is still salvation for one who has so long lived a careless life.'

"She then briefly told me her story. She was a person held in high esteem in the society in which she moved. But she was living without God and without Christ in the world and was entirely given up to pleasure and love of dress and display. Church or chapel she seldom or never visited. The places which she frequented were the theater and the ballroom. But on this Sunday morning, having gone out for a walk, her attention was struck by the singing which reached her ears from my chapel. The thought occurred to her that she might as well step in and sit down with the congregation. But here she found that she had come just in time to learn what the glory of man is. My sermon went like a two-edged sword through her heart. She saw that with all her beauty she was but a withering flower—dead, lost, helpless, and hopeless. And she now besought me to tell her more about that Saviour whom I had spoken of as the only One who was able to save from ruin.

"I need not tell you," my friend continued, "how gladly I told her of Christ. Her eyes were opened to the glory of His holiness. It was not long before she became a member of my church, and on that occasion she presented me with this picture."

"And what became of your sermons?" I asked archly.

"Well," he answered with a smile, "the Lord had taught me this great lesson, which I hope I have never forgotten since; namely, that oratory, rhetoric, etc., may be excellent things in a pulpit, but that without the eloquence of the Holy Spirit, which tells us of the love of Him who died for our sins, they will never lead a lost sinner to the fold of the only Good Shepherd."

Mortality

Oh, who can view the wasted flower,
  The naked field, the dying leaf,
When autumn winds proclaim their power,
  And still remain unmoved by grief!

An emblem this of man's career;
  His life's unfolding and decay;
He glories but a moment here,
  The fragile creature of a day.

Though dead, the floral tribes of spring
  Shall bloom, revived by fairer skies;
Like Phoenix, of unconquered wing,
  They'll from their lowly graves arise.

Child at Prayer

A few weeks since, in coming down the North River, I was seated in the cabin of the magnificent steamer *Isaac Newton* in conversation with some friends. It was becoming late in the evening, and one after another, seeking repose, made preparations to retire to their berths—some, pulling off their boots and coats and lying down to rest; while others, in the attempt to make it seem as much like home as possible, threw off more of their clothing—each one as his comfort or apprehension of danger dictated.

I had noticed on deck a fine looking boy, of about six years of age, following around a man evidently his father, whose appearance indicated him to be a foreigner, probably a German—a man of medium height and respectable dress. The child was unusually fair and fine looking, with handsome features and an intelligent and affectionate expression of countenance, and from under his German cap fell chestnut hair and thick, clustering curls.

After walking about the cabin for a time the father and son stopped within a few feet of where we were seated and commenced to prepare for going to bed. I watched them. While the little fellow was undressing himself, the father adjusted and arranged the bed the child was to occupy, which was upper berth. Having finished this, his father tied a handkerchief around the boy's head to protect his curls. This done I looked for him to seek his resting place. Instead of this, however, he quietly kneeled down upon the floor, put his little hands together in a beautifully childlike and simple manner, and resting his arms upon the lower berth against which he knelt, began his vesper prayer.

I listened and I could hear the murmuring of his sweet voice but could not distinguish the words he spoke. There were men around him—Christian men—retiring to rest without prayer; or, if praying at all, it was a kind of mental desire for protection, without sufficient courage or piety to kneel down in the steamboat's cabin and before strangers acknowledge the goodness of God asking His protection and love. This was the result of some pious mother's training. Where was she now? How many times had her kind hands been laid on the sunny locks as she had taught him to lisp his prayer.

A beautiful sight it was, that child at prayer, in the midst of the busy, thoughtless throng. He alone, of this worldly multitude, drew nigh to heaven. I thanked the parental love that had taught him to lisp his evening prayer and could scarcely refrain from weeping then, nor can I now, as I see again that sweet child, in the crowded tumult of the steamboat's cabin, bending in devotion before his Maker.

When the little boy had finished his evening prayer, he arose and kissed his father most affectionately, who then put him in his berth for the night. I felt a strong desire to speak to them, but deferred it till morning. When morning came the confusion of landing prevented me from seeing them again. But if ever I meet that boy in his happy youth, in his anxious manhood, in his declining years, I will thank him for the influence and example of the night's devotion, and bless the name of the mother who taught him.

Not Good. Not Bad.

"From what you have said, John, it seems you think yourself a fair kind of man."

"Well, Mr. F——, I will tell you my opinion about that exactly. I don't think I ever did much that was bad, nor can I say that I ever did a great deal of good. I think you may call me a middling man."

"That is your opinion, John. But don't you think that everything that exists must have had a cause from which it sprung?"

"Certainly I do, Mr. F——, for old John is not so void of sense as not to know that."

"Well, John, what do you suppose causes a man to be good?"

"God, of course, sir."

"And what do you think causes a man to be bad?"

"The devil, most certainly; for God never made anything bad."

"But John, what is the cause of a middling man?"

"W-e-ll, I sup-p-o-s-e——"

"John, I perceive you have got fast there. You say God is the cause of a good man, and Satan is the cause of a bad man, but you say you are neither! You are middling. Doubtless, John, you must have had a cause that made you what you are.

"But as there is no middle between God and Satan, and only the two revealed causes of good and evil in man, then I am at an exceedingly great loss to know what has been the great moral cause that made you middling."

"Why, sir, I have heard a great many folks like me saying that they were middling, that is, neither good nor bad; but, really, when I think of the matter in the way you put it, I begin to be somewhat doubtful whether I am right. Yet, I assure you, sir, I do not think I should be called a very bad man."

"John, did you ever see a middling gold dollar? Or did you ever see a middling banknote?"

"No, never, Mr. F——; they are always either good or bad. But I have known some bad ones to pass for good ones."

"Well, John, if you never saw middling money, you never saw middling men; that is, as before God. God is a being of perfect holiness, infinite purity, and he judges according to a perfect standard. To be accepted of Him we must be perfectly fitted for His approval. He cannot adopt middling men and call them good. You must be either righteous or unrighteous—either saint or sinner. A middling man has no existence in God's sight. So, friend John, I want you, when you go home, to think seriously on this matter. 'You cannot serve two masters.' At this moment you are either serving God or Satan. You cannot be a middling man. You have no middling cause, no middling life, no middling death, and no middling destiny!"

Reader, as I have said to John, so I say to you. You are, at this moment, either good or bad, righteous or unrighteous, in God's sight. You cannot be middling. You are either a child of God or a servant of the wicked one.

You are pardoned or unpardoned. You are either a subject of God's grace, or you are under His condemnation.

The Hermit and the Traveler

Once there lived in a castle a very wicked man, who despised the poor, oppressed the weak, and was cruel to all over whom he had power. He had armed soldiers to do his bidding; and as he was cruel and selfish, as well as powerful, he robbed the people who could not defend themselves. If any of them resisted, he burned their dwellings and laid waste their fields.

He had a wife and two children. His wife was so gentle and beautiful and his children so good and lovely that even this bad man prized them above all his possessions.

One day a man came to the castle and asked to see him. His garments were poor, like those worn by the peasants who till the soil; but his countenance was fierce, and his eye flashed with anger.

"Your soldiers have burned my house and carried away my wife, and I am here to demand justice!"

He spoke sternly. If this peasant had stooped and cringed to his powerful neighbor and asked justice as a favor, the soldiers might have been ordered to bring back his wife; but as it was, the wicked lord of the castle, who had no pity in his heart, fell into a great passion and, lifting his sword, tried to slay the poor man. Just at this moment his wife came into the apartment, leading her beautiful children, and seeing the sword in her husband's upraised hand, cried out in alarm.

At sight of these, his enemy's most precious things, the fires of hatred and revenge burned up fiercely in the peasant's heart, and drawing a concealed weapon he killed them with thrusts given as quick as lightning flashes. In the next moment he was gone, and the strong, bad man stood horror-stricken over his dead wife and children. All his wicked life crowded back upon his memory. The warning words of a pious man—"God's justice will find you out!"— scarcely noticed when spoken, now rang in his ears like tones of thunder. His soul was crushed under a weight of remorse and sorrow. A great terror oppressed him. He seemed standing face to face with an awful power he had scorned and defied.

From this time men lost sight of him. His castle fell into ruins, and weeds and briers covered all his neglected fields. Many years afterwards a traveler lost his way in a great forest. While vainly seeking his way out, he came upon a hermit, who lived in a rocky cave by the mouth of which ran a clear stream of water. He was dressed in poor garments; his beard was white and hung down almost to his waist; his face was thin, and his eyes sunken. The traveler's heart was filled with pity at the sight of so miserable a being.

"Who are you? And what are you doing here?" he asked.

"I have been a great sinner," said the hermit. "I was a cruel oppressor, a bold wrongdoer. I defied God, and He laid His hand heavily upon me. Then I fled away from the sight of men to this wilderness that I might repent and punish myself. My food has been herbs instead of dainty meats; my drink water instead of rich wines. I spend long nights in prayer; I cut my body with stripes until it is covered with wounds. And though I have done all this for years, yet God still hides Himself from me in anger. My sins have been too great. He will not forgive! Oh, that I had not been born!"

"Wretched man," said the traveler, "God hides Himself from no one. It is you that have hidden yourself from God. He dwells here with the happy birds, with the fragrant blossoms, and pure running water—with all nature in her orderly work—but not with man idly bemoaning himself. If you wish to find God, go where His poor, His suffering and needy ones are, and join Him in helping them."

The hermit covered his face and sank down upon the ground. All strength went out of his limbs. He was weak and helpless as a little child.

"Begin a new and truer life," continued the traveler, "by at once showing me the way out of this forest. I have much work to do for God among the children of men, and they suffer loss while I am away."

The hermit rose from the ground slowly, as strength came back to him, and silently led the traveler out of the forest.

"Prayer and fastings and self-denials are all vain," said the traveler, as they stood still on the great high-road, "unless there be good deeds. Go back among your fellowmen and do them good if you desire God's favor; you will never find it here."

After ten year's absence, the lord of the castle came back to its desolate walls. His hair was white as wool; his form wasted and bent; his countenance thin and sorrowful. Men stood aloof from him, for they remembered how wicked and cruel he had been. The weak trembled at his return, for they feared his oppression.

Soon the hearts of all began to turn to the lord of the castle; for instead of doing evil, as before, his hand was showing itself in good works. He kept no soldiers to guard his gates and defend him from enemies, for he had no enemies. The poor were helped, the sick cared for, and the vicious restrained. He was a father and protector of the people.

One day, as he sat looking from the window of his castle at the peaceful country which lay all around him, peaceful and happy because he was on the side of good instead of evil, he saw the traveler who had been lost in the forest passing by, and he sent his servant after him. When the two men stood face to face the traveler said, "Have we not met before?"

And the lord of the castle answered, "Yes, you came to me once with a message from God."

Then the traveler knew him, and his countenance was full of gladness; for, in place of the miserable, self-afflicted hermit, he saw a peaceful old man whose life of good deeds had brought him so near God that his face was as the face of an angel in its tranquil sweetness.

"God hears you now," said the traveler.

"He is very near. He fills my heart with His love. I am His servant," answered the lord of the castle, bowing his head with a great reverence.

"Ah, yes," said the traveler. "It is the faithful servant who worships God in well-doing that gets the blessing. Others never find it."

Then they broke bread and prayed together, and the traveler went on his way, rejoicing that the good seed sown by the wayside had yielded so rich a harvest.

Peter Crisp's Spectacles

Peter Crisp had something the matter with his eyes; he needed spectacles to help him see. But this was no uncommon misfortune; hundreds of people, who do ten good hours' work every day of their lives, use glasses and cannot get along without them. No, the chief trouble in Peter's case was not in wanting glasses; it was in the particular sort of glasses that he used. He had several pairs, which he always kept on hand, nobody knew exactly where; they seemed to be hidden somewhere about the head of his bed, for he often got them on before he was up in the morning.

One pair was what I should call smoked glasses, such as persons use in looking at the sun; they do very well for that purpose, preventing the bright rays from hurting the eyes. But Peter did not put them on to look at the sun with; he looked at everything through them. And as this made everything look dark and ugly, he was made to feel so accordingly.

"I could iron these collars better myself!" he exclaimed one morning as he was dressing, after getting up with those glasses on. And a few minutes after, "Not a pin in the cushion as usual!" and presently again, "Who *has* taken my comb and brush?"

Had any of the children chanced to come into the room about that time, it would have been worse for them.

When he sat down to breakfast there was a deep wrinkle between his eyes, caused by the weight of his glasses upon his brow.

"That Polly Ann never did make a good cup of coffee in her life," he remarked. "My dear," turning to his wife, "I do wish you would take the trouble to go down once—just once, *only* once—and show her how."

Mrs. Crisp ventured to say in a low voice that she went down every morning. Peter had no reply to make to this, but he puckered his lips as if he had been taking quinine, frowned yet more severely, and pushed the cup away from him.

After his cheerful breakfast he put on his hat to go to the store but turned back from the front door and came to the foot of the stairs, where he stood calling out in a loud voice that he really felt ashamed of the black around the doorknob and bell handle. In the street a few moments afterward, a gentleman joined him, to whom he was as pleasant as possible. But when he got into the counting room, it was plain he had the smoked glasses on still. Not one person about the concern worked as he should, he said, none of them were worth a cent. It used to be different when he was a boy. Then he went out with a look of general disgust. As soon as he was gone the bookkeeper was cross to the clerk, and the clerk scolded the boy, and the boy went out and abused the porter.

A few mornings after that, Peter had on what might be called his blue glasses. He was in milder frame but low in spirits. He was sorry to see the chamber carpet wearing out, for he did not know where another one would come from. At breakfast he watched all the children taking butter and took scarcely any himself. He begged Mrs. Crisp to put less sugar in his coffee. The frown was gone from his face, but a most dejected look had come in its place. Spying a hole in the toe of his boy's shoe, he took a long breath; and hearing that the dressmaker was engaged a day next week for his daughters, he sighed aloud. Walking down the street, he looked as if he had lost a near relative, and at the store all day he felt like one on the eve of breaking.

He had one more pair of glasses, the color of which could never be distinctly made out; they seemed more of a mud-color than anything else. He did not wear them so often as either of the others, but when he did they had a very singular effect. It was thought by many that they befogged him rather than helped him to see, for after putting them on of a morning he would get up and dress hardly speaking a word. At breakfast he would say nothing and not seem to want anybody else to; consequently the whole family would rise from the table and walk out of the front door as if he were dumb. Although it was a relief when he had gone and made matters something better, still a chilling influence remained behind him the whole morning.

Peter had been wearing these glasses a good many years, when it occurred to him one day that things never looked very cheerful in his eyes, that he was never very happy, and that perhaps his spectacles had something to do with it.

"I wish I could get another and a better pair," said he. Then he remembered that his neighbor, Samuel Seabright, had to wear glasses also, but he always appeared to see well and to have a pleasant face. Meeting him the next morning, he said, "Neighbor, if it is not making too free, may I ask where you got your spectacles?"

"Certainly," replied Samuel. "I am glad to tell you. They are good ones, and I wish every man with poor eyes had a pair like them."

"I would be willing to pay a good price for a pair," said Peter.

"That is not needful," replied Samuel; "they are the cheapest glasses you can get."

"Pray tell me where I can find them," said Peter.

"I got mine," said Samuel, "by the help of a certain physician whose house you pass every day; and if you are truly anxious to get them, I know he will tell you how you can get a pair for the asking."

"I don't want them in charity," replied Peter.

"Then you cannot have them," said Samuel.

"Well," replied Peter, in a humbler voice, "I'll take them for nothing or I'll pay a big price for them, for I want them above all things."

"Ah," said Samuel, "that sounds more like getting them. You go to him and tell him how you feel, and he will tend to your case."

Then Peter did as he was told. The doctor looked at his eyes, and said that the disease in them was one which kept him from seeing the good things about him; all he could see was the evil.

"And those glasses you have been wearing," he continued, "have only made them worse, till there is danger of your getting beyond cure."

"And is there no hope for me?" asked Peter.

"Oh yes," replied the doctor, "if you will follow the directions."

"I will do so," said Peter.

"In the first, then," he continued, "you must wear those glasses no more. Throw them away or put them in the fire, so that you will never see them again."

"I promise to do so," replied Peter.

"In the next place, when you are given a new pair," continued the doctor, "you must walk in the way which they show you to be right."

"I will try not to depart from it," said Peter.

At this there came an invisible hand that took off his old smoked glasses and put on new ones, made of pure crystal, which let the light through just as it came down from the sky. But oh, what a change they made to Peter! He went home, and as soon as he entered the door his house seemed like another place to him; it seemed filled with blessings.

"Is it possible," he exclaimed, "that those glasses have kept me from seeing all these before?"

The next morning when he got up he told his wife what had befallen him and how he felt in consequence.

"But," said she, with a loving smile, "how about those badly ironed collars, and the pins, and the weak coffee?"

"Oh," he cried, "how could I ever let such trifles trouble me?"

"And then," she continued, "here is the carpet wearing out and the boys' shoes and the girls' dresses."

"As for them, we will hope to get more when they are gone. But even if we should not have half of our present comforts and indulgence, with you, my dearest, and our precious children about me, I trust I may feel too rich ever again to utter one complaining word."

So the sunshine came into Peter Crisp's house, and he and all his family led a happier life because of his new glasses, which were, a thankful heart.

Stick to Your Business

There is nothing which should be more frequently impressed upon the minds of young men than the importance of steadily pursuing some one business. The frequent changing from one employment to another is one of the most common errors committed, and to it may be traced more than half the failures of men in business and much of the discontent and disappointment that render life uncomfortable. It is a very common thing for a man to be dissatisfied with his business and to desire to change it for some other, which, it seems to him, will prove more lucrative; but in nine cases out of ten, it is a mistake.

Here is a young man who commenced life as a mechanic, but from some cause imagined that he ought to have been a doctor. So after a hasty and shallow preparation, he has taken up the saddlebags only find that work is still work, that his patients are no more profitable than his workbench, and that the occupation is not a whit more agreeable.

Here are two young men—clerks; one of them is content, when his first term of service is over, to continue a clerk till he shall have saved enough to commence business on his own account. The other can't wait, but starts off without capital, and with a limited experience, and brings up after a few years in a court of insolvency, while his former comrade, by patient perseverance, comes out at last with a fortune.

That young lawyer, who became disheartened because briefs and cases did not crowd upon him while he was yet redolent of calf-bound volumes and had small use for red tape concluded he had mistaken his calling and so plunged into politics. He finally settled down into the character of a middling pettifogger, scrambling for his daily bread.

There is an honest farmer who has toiled a few years, got his farm paid for, but does not grow rich very rapidly, as much for lack of contentment mingled with his industry as anything, though he is not aware of it. He hears the wonderful stories of some far-off land and how fortunes may be had for the trouble of picking them up, mortgages his farm to raise money, goes away, and after many months of hard toil, comes home to commence again at the bottom of the hill for a more weary and less successful climbing up again.

Mark the men in every community who are notorious for ability and equally notorious for never getting ahead, and you will usually find them to be those who never stick to any one business long but are always forsaking their occupation just when it begins to be profitable.

Young men, stick to your business. It may be you have mistaken your calling. If so, find it out as quickly as possible and change it, but don't let any uneasy desire to get along fast, or a dislike of your honest calling, lead you to abandon it. Have some honest occupation and then stick to it; pursue the business you have chosen persistently, industriously, and hopefully. And if there is anything of you, it will appear and turn to account in that, as well as, or better than, in any other calling. Only if you are a loafer, forsake that line as speedily as possible, for the longer you stick to it the worse it will stick to you.

"That's Thee, Jem!"

A band, or "troupe," of young men, with hands and faces blackened and dressed in very grotesque costumes, arranged themselves one day for an exhibition of their peculiar "performances," before the door of an earnest Christian merchant, whom we will call Mr. Carr, who resided in a noted English watering place. After they had sung some comic and plaintive melodies, with their own peculiar accompaniments of gestures and grimaces, one of the party, a tall and interesting young man, who had the "look" of one who was beneath his proper station, stepped up to the door, tambourine in hand, to ask for a few "dropping pennies" of the people. Mr. Carr, taking a Bible from his window, which he kept there for sale, addressed the youth, "See here, young man, I will give you a shilling, and this Book besides, if you will read a portion of it among your comrades there, and in the hearing of bystanders."

"Here's a shilling for an easy job!" he chuckled out to his mates; "I'm going to give you a 'public reading!'"

Mr. Carr opened at the fifteenth of Luke, and, pointing to the eleventh verse, requested him to commence there.

"Now, Jem, speak up!" said one of the party, "and earn your shilling like a man!"

Jem took the Book and read "'And he said, "A certain man had two sons; and the younger of them said to his father, 'Father, give me the portion of goods that falleth to me.' And he divided unto them his living.""'"

There was something in the voice of the reader, that lulled all to silence while an air of seriousness took possession of the youth and commanded the rapt attention of the crowd.

He read on: "'And not many days after, the younger son gathered all together and took his journey into a far country, and there wasted his substance with riotous living.'"

"That's *thee*, Jem!" ejaculated one of his comrades, "it's just like what you told me of yourself and your father!"

Jem continued: "'And when he had spent all, there arose a mighty famine in that land; and he began to be in want.'"

"Why, that's *thee* again, Jem!" said the voice. "Go on!"

"'And he went and joined himself to a citizen of that country, and he sent him into his fields to feed swine. And he would fain have filled his belly with the husks that the swine did eat; and no man gave unto him.'"

"That's like us all!" said the voice, once more interrupting. "We are all *beggars;* and might be better than we are! Go on; let's hear what came of it!"

The young man read on with a trembling voice: "'And when he came to himself, he said, "How many hired servants of my father's have bread enough and to spare, and I perish with hunger! I will arise and go to my father."'"

At this point he fairly broke down and could read no more. All were impressed and moved. The whole reality of the past rose up to view; and, in the clear story of the gospel, a ray of hope dawned upon him for his future. His father—his father's house—and his mother, too; and the plenty and the love ever bestowed upon him there; and the hired servants, all having enough; and then *himself*, his father's *son;* and his present state, his companionship, his habits, his sins, his poverty, his outcast condition, all these came climbing, like an invading force, into the citadel of his mind and fairly overcame him.

That day—that scene—provided the turning point of that young prodigal's life. He sought advice of Mr. Carr, communications were made to his parents, and the long-lost and dearly loved child returned to the familiar earthly home; and, still better, to his heavenly Father! He found the promises of the parable of the prodigal son true both for time and for eternity.

> Yes, there is One who will not chide nor scoff,
> But beckons us to homes of heavenly bliss;
> Beholds the prodigal a great way off,
> And flies to meet him with a Father's kiss!

The Widow's Mite

During the winter of 1846 I went with John H. W. Hawkins and Dr. Charles Jewett to Woodford, where we were to both hold a temperance meeting and organize a Washingtonian Society. The weather was favorable, the sleighing excellent, and the meetings were large and of the most enthusiastic character. People came from many miles around, and we had the pleasure of seeing large and vigorous society springing into existence.

The first day, while Mr. Hawkins was telling his experience of sorrow and misfortune from the intoxicating cup, I noticed a poorly clad, middle-aged woman, who wept and sobbed as though her heart would break. At the close of the meeting that woman was among the first to place her name to the pledge. When she had laid down the pen and returned to her seat, I looked to see what she had written. It was a tremulous hand but delicate and exceedingly well formed, and the name she had written was "Bertha Morrison."

"Poor woman!" said the newly elected president, when I asked him if he knew her. "Her's has been a hard, sad fate. Once she was the fairest and most blithesome of all the maidens of Woodford. She married Tom Morrison, a brave, impetuous, handsome fellow—a sailor upon the lake, and for a time she was the happiest of the happy. But the demon came, and joy was gone. One child, a boy, had been born to them—born to shame and misery. Tom sank lower and lower, until he finally dropped into a drunkard's grave.

Her son ran away and went to sea, and when she last heard of him he was on shore in a distant city, running a wild race of riot and dissipation. She has put forth every exertion in her power to save him, but thus far he has avoided her. She has not been able even to see him. Still, he is not entirely evil. He has sent her money several times. Once he met a man in New York, who was coming to Woodford, and by him he sent to his mother the last shilling he possessed and then went and shipped for a voyage to India."

The president would have told me more but his attention was called to business, and I was left to reflect upon what I had heard.

Our last meeting was on Saturday evening at the close of which a collection was taken up for the benefit of the secretary. I had been watching the poor widow, and I was still looking that way when the contribution box was passed down the slip in which she sat. She spoke to the collector, and I saw her drop a piece of money. When the box was brought to the desk I asked the man what Bertha Morrison had said to him.

"She told me," he replied, with moistening eyes and quivering lip, "that she gave the last mite she possessed in the world, and she hoped God would bless it. She had kept it because her son had sent it to her. It was an English shilling, and her boy had sent it when it was the sum of all he had in his purse."

I asked the man if he could distinguish the piece. He said he could because it was the only piece of the kind in the box, and directly afterward he brought it to me. It was bright, with the stamp fresh and unworn, and upon the side bearing the crown I noticed the letters, "D.M." cut in as though with the point of a knife. I gave the collector a silver dollar and kept the widow's mite. I not only prized it for its touching associations, but I meant to make it a symbol of devotion in my appeals in the future to my fellows.

This was in the winter. During the next autumn I was in Baltimore, where I visited the penitentiary for the purpose of conversing with those poor unfortunates whom love of strong drink had dragged down to those prison depths.

"There's about the toughest case we've got," said the warden, pointing to a man who sat upon a low bench in a corner engaged in making a boat sail.

I gained a position where I could see the man's face. He was young—not much more than two or three and twenty—and the face was one that attracted me. He had been a month in the institution, the track of the demon was gone, and the hue of health had come in its place. I could judge that he was self-willed and not to be driven; but there was native goodness beneath the surface, and I was sure that in his bosom was throbbing a great and generous heart. I felt strangely drawn toward the young man, and at length I asked the warden if he would send him to his cell and permit me to be alone with him there. Consent was cheerfully given, and the turnkey was called and directed to conduct the prisoner away. Meantime I had been informed that the man's name was John Thompson, and he was a sailor. He had been imprisoned as a common drunkard.

I entered the prisoner's cell, and the door was closed and locked behind me. I took a seat, at the same time extending a cheerful salutation.

"Look here, mate," he said resolutely, but with not a particle of impudence, "if you've come here to preach, you're on the wrong track. I don't want to hear a word—not a word!"

I told him I was not a preacher—that I once followed the sea and had been a poor unfortunate victim of strong drink. At first his face grew bright with sympathy, and then it darkened again.

"So you've come to talk temperance to me?" he said, somewhat bitterly.

"Not if you object," I replied. "But I have come to see if you do not think there is something in you of good worth saving. You've been drifted upon a lee shore, that's all. Why not down helm, brace up sharp, go about, and stand off? There's plenty of sea room left."

And then I told him a story of a narrow escape I once had from a lee shore in a gale of wind, off the coast of Sicily. Finally I led him to tell me some of his adventures, and it thus came out that I found him to possess not only rare intelligence but a rich fund of sense and humor.

By-and-by I ventured to ask him concerning his friends and relatives, and after much effort I gained from him that all his near relatives were dead save his mother.

"And sh—she—may be dead before this!" he said. "But, if she still lives, she has forgotten me." He tried to speak calmly and as one who feels but little concern; but his heart was too much for him, and his speech faltered, and he rested his brow upon his hand.

"Ah," said I, "you little heed a mother's love when you say that."

And then, as exactly and peculiarly fitted for the occasion, I told him the story of the poor widow and her mite. I told it feelingly and with earnest zeal. He buried his face in his hands, and I saw the tears trickle down between his fingers. His frame shook; and once he was so mightily convulsed that I stopped, but he recovered and I went on.

"Where was it?" he asked in a broken whisper, when I concluded.

"In the town of Woodford," I told him.

"And the widow's name?"

"Bertha Morrison."

"Did you say that you had that piece of money now?" He looked up, and his face was like marble. The tide of life seemed to have set back into his heart.

I told him I had it, and I took it from my purse and handed it to him. He looked at it—turned it over and examined where the letters had been cut in with a knife. And then his heart swelled, and the surging flood burst forth. He wept and sobbed, and called, "Mother! Mother! Mother!" Finally, in broken accents, he said, "I sent her this! It was my last shilling! And when I sent it I prayed that God would turn it to some blessing for my poor mother. I am here under a false name—I am Donald Morrison."

Again he sobbed until his heart seemed ready to burst within him, and when he next looked up he stretched forth his hand imploringly.

"Leave me! Oh, go away for a time and leave me to myself! Leave me a little while, and then come back. Let me keep this."

I called the turnkey and went out, and to him and the warden I told what had transpired. They were both kindhearted men and were deeply affected.

In half an hour I went back and found the prisoner upon his knees, with his head bowed upon the edge of his cot. He arose as I entered and extended his hand.

"Please don't talk to me now," he said. "I can't bear it; I am too full."

"But," I ventured—for I had received encouragement from the warden, "suppose I could get you out from here, could let you breathe heaven's free air, with liberty to go where you pleased?"

He grasped my arm, and a new glory was on his handsome face.

"Oh, if you could do that I should be saved! You would give to my mother a son!"

That evening I went with the warden and saw the judge who passed the sentence, and with him we visited the mayor. I told my story, and in a few hours Morrison was free and jubilant. After a time he took my hand and said, "I know they have given me into your care. The warden told me so. I want to go alone. I don't want them to know of this until you have proved to them what I can be. You have given me back my manhood, and I now ask you to trust it. I will write to you—I will write you everything as it is. Will you trust me?"

I trusted him, and I was glad to do it; for it would have taken a week of my time to have accompanied him home, and my engagements were just then pressing. Five years had passed before I visited Woodford. I took dinner at the hotel and then sauntered forth in quest of my friends. At the first corner I inquired of a gentleman if he could tell me where the Widow Morrison lived. He said she lived about a half a mile away in a cottage by the lakeshore.

"But," he added, "you need not go so far to see her. She went into that store but a few moments since." And he pointed to a dry goods store across the way, before which stood a new and handsome carriage. "Ah, there she comes."

I looked and saw a woman, but not the woman I had known. The woman was blooming and handsome and seemed yet young.

"I spoke of Mrs. Bertha Morrison," I said.

"And that's she," pursued the gentleman. "Aye— and there is her son. Perhaps you haven't heard—" I lost the rest of the sentence. I had turned to look at the man who had followed the lady from the store—one of the grandest looking men I had ever seen. Our eyes met, and he recognized me. For an instant he was like one transfixed, but he quickly recovered himself. He handed the lady into the carriage, and then came over to me.

"God bless you!" he ejaculated, "I am glad you have come at last. But my mother must not see you here. It would be too much for her. Go to the hotel and wait there; I will come for you very soon."

As I walked back, the gentleman whom I had met upon the corner walked with me.

I asked him if he was acquainted with Donald Morrison. He said he was. Could he tell me what Mr. Morrison was doing?

"He's making a new town of Woodford!" exclaimed my companion, enthusiastically. "Five years ago he hired a little schooner and used to run down to Erie, and

Cleveland, and so on up to the Michigan shore. By-and-by he bought the schooner, and before the year was out he paid for it and took another. Today he owns three of the best steamboats on the lake."

In less than an hour Donald Morrison drove up to the door of the hotel, and I went home with him. The next hour was a chaos of joy and blessing. I cannot remember clearly what transpired.

I only know that we wept together like children, and that both mother and son clung to me as the source of their salvation and happiness.

I spent almost a month at the lakeshore cottage. They would not let me go sooner, nor would they let me go, even then, until I had promised that I would come to see them every summer and oftener if I could do so.

I still keep the widow's mite, and the blessing of God rests upon it. Many a poor wanderer in the way of sin and shame has been turned back into the path of honor and true manhood through the influence of its simple and touching story.

Help the Erring

Would'st thou an erring soul redeem,
  And lead a lost one back to God;
Would'st thou a guardian angel seem
  To one who long in guilt hath trod?
Go kindly to him—take his hand,
  With gentle words—within thine own;
And by his side a brother stand,
  Till thou the demon, sin, dethrone.

Scorn not the guilty, then, but plead
  With him, in kindest, gentlest mood,
And back the lost one thou mayest lead
  To God, humanity and good!
Thou art thyself but man, and thou
  Art weak, perchance to fall as he;
Then mercy to the fallen show,
  That mercy may be shown to thee!

The King and the Farmer

King Frederick of Prussia, when out riding one day, saw an old farmer, who was plowing a field and singing cheerfully over his work.

"You must be well off, old man," cried the king. "Does this acre belong to you on which you so industriously labor?"

"No, sir," replied the old man, who of course had no idea that he was speaking to the king; "I am not so rich as that. I plow for wages."

"How much do you earn a day?" asked the king.

"Eight groscehn," returned the man. That would be about twenty cents of our money.

"That is very little," said the king. "Can you get along with it?"

"Get along! Yes, indeed, and have something left."

"However do you manage?"

"Well," said the farmer, smiling, "I will tell you. Two groschen are for myself and my wife; with two I pay my old debts, two I lend, and two I give away for the Lord's sake."

"This is a mystery which I cannot solve," said the king.

"Then I must solve it for you," replied the farmer. "I have two old parents at home, who kept me and cared for me when I was young and weak and needed care. Now that they are old and weak, I am glad to keep and care for them. That is my debt, and it costs me two groschen a day to pay it. Two more I spend on my children's schooling. If they are living when their mother and I are old, they will keep us and pay back what I lend. Then with my last two groschen I support my two sick sisters, who cannot work for themselves. Of course I am not compelled to give them the money, but I do it for the Lord's sake."

"Well done, old man," cried the king, as he finished. "Now I am going to give you something to guess. Have you ever seen me before?"

"No," said the farmer.

"In less than five minutes you shall see me fifty times, and carry in your picket fifty of my likenesses."

"This is indeed a riddle which I cannot guess," said the farmer.

"Then I will solve it for you," returned the king, and with that he put his hand into his pocket and, pulling out fifty gold pieces, placed them in the hands of the farmer.

"The coin is genuine," said the king, "for it also comes from our Lord God, and I am His paymaster. I bid you good-bye."

And he rode off, leaving the good old man overwhelmed with surprise and delight.

Worth Better than Show

A young oriental prince was visiting at the castle of a duke in one of the finest countries of England. He looked from his window into a beautiful garden and inhaled the fragrance which was wafted toward him by the gentle breath of June.

"What exquisite perfume," he cried. "Bring me, I pray you, the flower that so delights my sense. See that stately stalk, bearing on its shaft those gorgeous lilies, whose snowy petals are veined with bloodred lines and with violet shade; that is undoubtedly the plant I seek."

They brought him the curious lily of Africa.

"Its odor is nauseating," he said, "but bring me that flower of a hue so much deeper and richer than even the beautiful roses of my own fair land. See how it glows like flame! Surely a rich odor should distill from the regal plant."

It was a dahlia, and its scent was even less agreeable than that of the lily.

"Can it be, then, the large white blossoms cluttered on yonder bush, or the blue cups on the neighboring shrub?" he asked.

No, the snowball and campanular proved alike scentless. Various plants yielded their odorless buds or broad-spreading petals for his inspection. But he found not among them what he sought.

"Surely, it must be that golden ball," he said, "for so showy a blossom should at least charm the nostrils as well as the eye."

"Faugh!" It was a marigold.

At length they placed in his hand a wee brown blossom.

"So unpretending a thing as this cannot surely be that for which I seek," exclaimed the prince with a vexed air. "This appears to be nothing better than a weed."

He cautiously lifted it to his face.

"Is it possible?" he cried. "Is it really this unobtrusive brown weed which gives forth so precious an odor? Why, it hangs over the whole garden, and comes fanning in at my window like the very breath of health and purity. What is the name of this little darling?"

"Precisely, that, your highness," answered his attendant; "this flower is called 'mignonette,' the little darling."

"Wonderful! Wonderful!" repeated the astonished prince, placing it in his bosom.

"Thus your highness perceives," remarked his tutor, gravely, "that the humble and unpretending often exhale the most precious virtues."

True Greatness

It naught avails thee where, but what thou art.
All the distinctions of this little life,
Are quite cutaneous, foreign in to the man—
Away with all but moral, in his mind;
And let what then remains compose his name,
Pronounce him weak or worthy, great or mean.
Th' Almighty, from His throne, on earth surveys
Naught greater than an honest, humble heart;
An humble heart, His residence! Pronounced
His second seat; and rival to the skies—
The private path, the secret acts of men,
If noble, far the noblest of our lives.

A Legacy

When Enoch Wilton died, people said that Daniel Naylor was sure to come into the possession of a handsome property, since Uncle Enoch was known to be rich, and Daniel was his favorite nephew.

But when the will came to be read, they changed their minds, for the only clause it contained relating to him read as follows: "And to Daniel Naylor, my beloved nephew, I give and bequeath, the framed copy of the temperance pledge to which under Divine Providence, I owe salvation from a drunkard's grave as well as all the material prosperity which has gladdened my latter years.   And I recommend that he remove it from its frame and affix his signature beneath mine, satisfied that he will find the pledge an unfailing source of wealth to him, as it has been to me."

Daniel Naylor resented this, as he was a drinking man, and he indignantly stowed away his uncle's bequest, among the old rubbish in the attic, assuring his wife that as his uncle had treated him so shabbily, he should not trouble himself further about that piece of property anyway.   So there, for years, it slumbered utterly forgotten.

Meanwhile, Daniel Naylor's affairs went from bad to worse, for his drinking habits had deepened their hold upon him.   One day, about five years subsequent to his uncle's death, he returned to his now squalid home to tell his wife that the last cent of his little property had gone, and that "Squire Grip," the village lawyer, would, the next day, foreclose the mortgage upon their little place, leaving them homeless.

"Oh, Daniel," exclaimed the poor woman in a tone of despair, "What shall we do? Where can we go?"

"I do not know," he responded moodily, "to the poorhouse, perhaps."

"Don't say that, Daniel!" pleaded the wife, "you still have two hands left, and if—"

"I cannot get employment," he interrupted. "I have been to all my employers, and they only shake their heads and say they are sorry but the times are so hard they cannot give me work. I shall have to give it up."

"But you must not give it up; there must be employment somewhere."

"I am unable to find it."

His wife paused a moment in deep reflection.

"If I will tell you how you can find employment, will you promise to fulfill the conditions necessary to obtain it?" she asked at length, in a very solemn tone.

"What are the conditions?"

"Will you promise?"

"I would rather know the conditions first."

"The conditions are that you quit your habits of intoxication and sign the temperance pledge."

Daniel Naylor started.

"What!" he cried in astonishment. "Do you intend to say that my having an occasional spree interferes with my obtaining work?"

"It certainly does, Daniel," was the sorrowful reply, "for I have heard at least one of your employees say as much."

"Who was it?"

"Mr. Field."

"What did he say?"

"You recollect the time about three weeks ago, when you were—were—"

"Drunk."

"Yes, when you were drunk. You were at work for him then, and when he came after you and I told him you could not come, he guessed the truth. Then I heard him say to his clerk, who accompanied him, as he drove off, 'Well, this is the *second* time Dan Naylor has failed me when I needed him most, but I shall be sure he does not do it again.' And that, my husband, is the source of all our adversity, as I believe you, yourself, will admit when you think the matter over."

It was Daniel Naylor's turn to reflect now, and for a few moments he did vigorously.

"Well, I believe you are right," he said, at last. "But what can I do now? Our home is gone, and I have lost the confidence of my employers, so signing the pledge cannot amount to much."

"Yes, it would amount to a great deal," his wife replied. "It would restore your self-respect, and in a great measure you would be able to regain the confidence you have forfeited."

Here was another period of silence and then looking up he cried, "Bring me a paper, and *I will sign it*, and may God give me the strength to keep it!"

"Why not sign Uncle Enoch's pledge?" his wife inquired. "I saw it lying up in the attic the other day, and if you wish I will bring it."

"Certainly, that will save writing another."

The pledge was soon brought, and Daniel Naylor received it from the frame and placed it upon the table. As he did so, a roll of brown paper fell out of its back and dropped unnoticed at his feet.

His name was speedily appended to the document, and then he turned to replace it in the frame.

In doing this, his eye fell upon the small parcel of brown paper lying on the floor.

Stooping to pick it up, he uttered a sudden cry of astonishment as he beheld the corner of a banknote protruding. And with fingers trembling with emotion, he undid the package to find *seven one thousand dollar notes*, and a scrap of paper on which was written: "Is not the pledge a sure road to wealth?"

"God bless good Uncle Enoch!" he exclaimed fervently. "I can now take up the mortgage, and as for the pledge, I will keep that sacred as long as I shall live, for my own sake as well as in gratitude for this timely assistance."

And his wife responded with a fervent "Amen."

Memory of the Just

As mid the ever rolling sea,
The Eternal Isles established be,
'Gainst which the billows of the main
Fret, rage, and break themselves in vain;

As in the Heavens, the urns divine
Of golden light forever shine;
Though clouds may darken, storms may rage,
They still shine on from age to age.

So, through the ocean tide of years,
The memory of the just appears;
So, through the tempest and the gloom,
The good man's virtues light the tomb.

Farmer Penniman's Dream

"There's no need of a donation for Mr. Goodman," growled out Mr. Penniman, on his way home from church, after the notice of a proposed donation visit had been given. "He has salary enough without—four hundred dollars a year and a parsonage and garden spot—that's enough for any family to live on. Why, it doesn't cost us near that, and we have six children; and they have only four. 'Twas real mean for Mr. Goodman to exchange, and get that man to give out the notice." And Mr. Penniman fretted away in the ear of his silent wife till they had nearly reached home, quite unmindful of the four children who, with wide open ears, were eagerly listening to every word.

Rev. Mr. Goodman was pastor of a little church in the small village of Manisuch, a Home Missionary church composed of farmers, with a few members in the village where two other churches of different denominations were also endeavoring to live and thrive.

Four hundred dollars was the nominal salary of Mr. Goodman from the Home Missionary Society. Of the four hundred Mr. Penniman gave twenty-five dollars, usually in advance, "to get it off his mind" he said—if all the subscribers had followed his example, it would have been better for the minister. But the last year's subscription was two hundred dollars in arrears. And the Home Missionary Treasury was empty.

It was mid-winter; the minister's credit and provisions were well exhausted, and nothing had been said of the accustomed donation visit.

Driven almost to desperation, Mr. Goodman rode over to a neighboring city, where one of his classmates was preaching to a large, prosperous church, and laid the case before him.

"Let's exchange," said the sympathizing listener, when the story was told. "I'll give notice of a donation visit on my own responsibility." The exchange was made, and the notice was given to the astonishment of everyone, Mrs. Goodman included.

Mr. Penniman's family went into their large, warm kitchen, laid aside their wrappings, and sat down to a bountiful dinner, prepared by the eldest daughter during their absence.   With the appearance of the hot mince pies began the discussion of the coming donation visit.

"Mother, may I go?" came from a chorus of little voices, and comments from the elder members of the family according to their moods.

"Well, I paid the whole of my subscription long ago," said Mr. Penniman, with a satisfied air, "and if the rest had done the same, there would be no excuse for having a donation visit."

"I don't believe Mr. Jones has paid a cent, and he's rich, too," said Clara, a bright little girl of eleven.

"No, nor Mr. White, nor Mr. Cook, nor even Deacon Slocum," added George, a stout lad of sixteen, who knew more, in his own estimation, than any man in the neighborhood.   Mrs. Penniman and the eldest daughter, Mabel, said nothing.

"Mother, I heard my teacher tell the superintendent that if people would only give tithes now, as the Jews did, there would be no need of donation parties. What are tithes?" said Robert, the nine-year-old son.

"I will tell you all about it this afternoon. Finish your dinner now," was the reply.

An hour later, according to promise, the mother sat, Bible in hand, explaining to her younger children the Jewish law of benevolence. Clara and Robert were finding the references, and James and Minnie were asking numberless questions. Jacob's vision interested them greatly. Robert read the dreamer's morning vow, "Of all that thou shalt give me, I will surely give the tenth unto thee."

"Then tithes mean tenths. Does it mean a tenth of everything?" asked Robert.

"Turn to Leviticus, chapter twenty-seven and verses thirty, thirty-one, and thirty-two," was the mother's reply.

"Why, mother, it says cattle, too," exclaimed Robert in astonishment, "and a tenth of all their grain and their fruit! Sure! I guess my teacher was right; but does anybody do that now-a-days?"

"Yes," replied Mrs. Penniman, "I have known several men in the city who conscientiously gave to the Lord one-tenth of their income, and some of them were far from rich."

"Why can't farmers do the same?" asked Clara.

"I suppose they might," replied the mother with a sigh. "Now turn to Malachi 3:8, 10."

"Let me read that," said Clara, and while she read, her father said to himself, "That's all right, I am glad my wife is so faithful in teaching the children, especially in teaching them benevolence. I guess I have paid my tithes this year; twenty-five dollars for Chicago, fifty dollars, that's a tenth and more too, but I don't begrudge it, not a bit," and with a self-satisfied smile he fell asleep and dreamed.

Half an hour passed, and the sleeper awoke with a groan and a start. Rousing himself, he said to the children, "Run away now and crack some nuts; I want to talk to your mother a while." The children obeyed, and the mother sat with folded hands, trying to prepare herself to listen patiently to more faultfinding.

"I have had such a fearful dream, Jennie," said Mr. Penniman, in a low, troubled voice, "a warning from God, I believe. You are a better Christian than I am, let me tell you my dream, and I know you will help me do my duty."

Then, in words often choked with emotion, he told his dream, while tears rolled down his wife's cheeks.

The profound silence which followed was broken by the husband's voice solemnly repeating the vow of Jacob, henceforth to be his own vow: "Of all that thou shalt give me I will surely give the tenth unto thee."

"Amen!" was the wife's joyful response.

"Isn't it Sabbath work to look over the books? It seems to me I shall feel better to have this matter all arranged today," said Mr. Penniman, after a few moment's thought.

Mrs. Penniman brought the books, in which her husband kept a full record of all the farm products.

"Now, Jennie," said he, "take a piece of paper, and as I call off the yield you take out the tenths, and we will estimate the value and see how much we fall short."

200 Bu. Wheat—tithes	20 Bu.	@	1.00	per	....	$20.00
150 " Potatoes "	15 "	@	0.60	"	....	9.00
300 " Oats "	30 "	@	0.30	"	....	9.00
600 " Corn "	60 "	@	0.28	"	....	16.80
200 " Apples "	20 "	@	0.50	"	....	10.00
10 " Beans "	1 "	@	1.50	"	....	1.50
30 " Turnips "	3 "	@	0.25	"	....	0.75
10 bbls. Beef "	1 bbl.	@	10.00	"	....	10.00
20 tons Hay "	2 tons	@	10.00	"	....	20.00

"The amount of tithes is $97.05" said Mrs. Penniman, "and deducting the $50.00 already paid here and for Chicago, leaves $47.05."

"Yes, that is correct," remarked Mr. Penniman, looking over the figures. "Now, how shall we arrange the rest? Let us see. We will give the minister one barrel of beef worth $10.00, and the tithes of turnips, beans and potatoes, which will amount to 11.25.

"The total $21.25 deducted from the $47.05 leaves $25.00, a little more than the price of two tons of hay, as we valued it. But we have not tithed our cattle yet; we have ten cows, you know—shall they 'pass under the rod?'" asked the husband, with a meaning smile.

"Yes, certainly," was the earnest reply.

"Well, then, one cow—you shall say which one— and two tons of hay to feed her on. There are a good many things we cannot tithe this year, so I will take a good large grist, and you may take what you like from the house, and next year we will be more exact," said Mr. Penniman in a tone of great satisfaction.

"A good deal to give away," said Mrs. Penniman, doubtingly, for in her heart she feared her husband would repent his liberality when the excitement of his dream had passed away.

"Why, Jennie, you are not sorry the Lord made the tenths so large, are you?" he said, half reproachfully. "Nine-tenths are left for us to use without doubt or reproach. How blind I have been all my life," he added, with a sigh.

"Father, George says it is milking time," called out little Clara, looking in at the door.

"Yes, I'll come," answered the father, rising. "Jennie, which cow shall I give," he asked, turning to his wife.

"Give the best to the Lord," was her reply.

"Mabel, come here a few minutes," said Mrs. Penniman to her eldest daughter, a young lady of nineteen, when the door had closed on the father and the two boys. In a few words the mother related what had transpired within the last hour, and the daughter listened with clasped hands and glistening eyes.

"Oh, mother, I am so glad!" she exclaimed. "Giving a tenth has always seemed right since I read God's own law to the Jews. He must know best. If the Jews were commanded to give tithes, surely, with our greater blessings, a tenth of our income is the very least we ought to think of presenting to the Lord as a thank offering. It seems a great deal because God gives us so much."

"Well, my dear, you and I must look up our tithes tomorrow," said Mrs. Penniman with a smile.

The day of the donation visit came at last.

"George, I guess we will take over our loads this morning," said Mr. Penniman while they were doing the chores at the barn. "You may fasten Brindle's rope to the back of that load of hay and let her eat while you help me load up the other sleigh. Then you may harness the old horses, I will take the colts, and we will go over together."

"Why, Father, what are you going to do with old Brindle?" asked the astonished boy.

"Give her to the minister; we have nine cows left," was the reply.

The two went to the house and proceeded to load up the "big sleigh" which stood before the door—a barrel of beef, potatoes, turnips, beans, and a "monstrous grist," the children said, and away the two drove to the parsonage.

"Why, Mr. Penniman, haven't you made a mistake? What does all this mean?" exclaimed Mr. Goodman running out of the house without his hat, as they drove through the great gate. "What does it all mean?"

"Only the tithes," replied Mr. Penniman, laughing.

"Here's your hat, Father," said little Henry Goodman, holding up the missing article. "Thank you, my son, now run into the house."

"Where shall I put your cow?" asked Mr. Penniman.

"My cow! Why, Mr. Penniman, you can't afford—"

"Got nine left," interrupted Mr. Penniman. "Drive on, George, we'll find a place."

The little barn was a rickety old affair, but Brindle was soon tied in one corner of the stable, and Mr. Penniman and his son stowed away the hay as best they could in the bay and shaky loft. The boards on the sides were some of them hanging by one nail, but George said that the roof looked as if it would not leak, and he would drive a few nails in those boards before night.

Then came the unloading of the second sleigh, amid exclamation of wonder and delight from Mr. and Mrs. Goodman and the children, and such a time as they all had preparing the little almost unused cellar for such an unexpected supply of vegetables.

Two empty barrels were filled to overflowing with the best flour, the bran and shorts for the cow found a place in some old barrels in the woodshed, and Mr. Penniman and George drove home delighted.

"What has happened to Mr. Penniman?" asked Mrs. Goodman after they had gone. "Is he going crazy?"

"I asked him what it all meant, and he said he had a dream last Sabbath which he would tell me sometime," replied her husband.

"The result of his dreaming will bless us all the year," said Mrs. Goodman gratefully.

"Mother, is that cow to be our very own, always?" asked one of the children.

"Yes. We all thank Mr. Penniman very much, and I am sure none of us will forget to thank Him who put the thought of this great kindness into Mr. Penniman's heart."

The afternoon and evening passed off as usual on such occasions, with one exception. The Penniman children had all faithfully tithed their nuts, popcorn, and the money in their savings banks, and brought their gifts to the children at the parsonage, and, childlike, Robert told the story to a group of listening children and some of larger growth.

"We are all tithed," said he, "George gave his tithes in money—Mother and Mabel brought butter and eggs and dried apples and ever so many cans of fruit, and Father tithed everything in the cellar and even tithed old Brindle, too."

"What is tithing? I don't know what you are talking about," said Willie Greene, the merchant's son.

"Why the Bible says folds must give to the Lord one-tenth of all they can raise on the farm," replied Robert. "Clara and I read it there last Sabbath, and that is just what we have been doing at our house. We have just begun, but we mean to keep on doing so all the time. I tell you, Henry Goodman, you'll get lots of eggs and chickens before the summer is out, and I shouldn't wonder if you should get, now and then, a harvest of apples. I have one tree that's all my own."

"That boy of yours has been telling quite a long story to the children about the tithing done at your house," remarked Mr. Stevens to Mr. Penniman when they went out after supper to attend to their teams. "Haven't you changed your mind lately?" he asked.

"Yes, I have most essentially," replied Mr. Penniman, "but it is a long story. Come to prayer meeting tomorrow evening, and you shall hear all about it."

Twenty minutes later everybody in the house knew that Mr. Penniman would explain the reason for the change in his feelings and practice at the next prayer meeting, and everyone had resolved to go tomorrow evening—not long to wait.

"Are you going to prayer meeting tonight to hear Penniman tell his dream?" asked Mr. Greene, the merchant, of the first customer who made his appearance the next morning.

"Yes. I want to hear what he will say. It seems silly, though, to talk about a dream doing such wonders, for his donation was large for anyone and certainly wonderful for him."

"A dream!" sneered Mr. Greene, brushing his coat-sleeve, "conscience, more likely."

"I don't know about that," was the reply; "Mr. Penniman is close, but he is honest and true to his word— always pays when and what he agrees to pay. His subscription is always paid in advance, if possible."

So passed the day; in every house and in every shop and store the subject of tithing was thoroughly discussed, always concluding with a wise shake of the head and the sage remark: "The Pennimans won't hold out long. No farmer can afford to give away one-tenth of what he raises, cattle and all." But they went to the prayer meeting, and for once the cold, cheerless little church was packed full.

Mr. Goodman opened the meeting as usual, and then remarked, "Brethren and friends, I know you are all anxious to hear the message which Brother Penniman brings us tonight, and we will listen to him now."

Slowly Mr. Penniman rose to his feet and looked around on the congregation. His face was deadly pale, and his lips quivered for a moment. Then, in a calm, distinct tone he said, "My first duty tonight is confession. I have frequently said, in the presence of many of you, my brethren, that our minister's salary was amply sufficient to support his family without donation parties—that he must be extravagant or he would not get into debt. Now, that was all wrong; I am sorry for it and ashamed of it. In the first place the statement was not true, though I did not intend to falsify. I made the mistake which we farmers are apt to make; we only reckon our money outlay and count as nothing what we consume.

"Yesterday, I took my books and deducted the amount of family supplies I had sold from the amount produced on my farm last year, and I was surprised. Now, I only wonder how, with the closest economy, our pastor's family could live comfortably on his salary and our donations too. But if my assertion had been true to the letter, it was no business of mine how he spent the money he had honestly earned, any more than it is how any other man spends the money he earns. The only question for me, as a member of this church, to decide is whether Mr. Goodman's labors among us are worth the salary which we agree to pay. If so, my portion of his salary is to be paid promptly and fully, like any other debt, and he and his family left to the expenditure of the money well and faithfully earned, without remark or hindrance. This shall always be my course toward him and every other pastor hereafter.

"Last Sabbath I sat in my easy chair, listening to my wife and children as they read and conversed about the Jewish law of tithing till I fell asleep with the very comfortable feeling that, for myself, I had brought all the tithes into the storehouse—and I really believed it.

"I dreamed that I went to the anticipated donation visit with my family and carried about my usual donation—a bushel of flour, a bag of potatoes, and a bag of apples—and thought I had done well, for I was very sure the minister did not need even that with his salary.

"The evening passed as usual, we farmers talking of the crops of last year and discussing our plans for the coming season. I was well satisfied to find, by comparison, how abundant my harvest had been.

"When I came in sight of my home, that night, I saw my well-filled barn in flames, my garnered treasures gone beyond hope of rescue. It was a terrible blow, and as I stood there helpless—for nothing could be done—and saw the product of my hard toil a great blazing mass, how I wished I had given more of that burning wheat to my pastor. But it was too late now. I had only enough left for bread and for seed—a few bushels put in another barn for lack of room.

"It was summer; my oats were sown; corn and potatoes planted; the cattle and sheep were in the pastures; but there was no rain. Day after day the sun arose without a cloud, and night after night the moon and stars shone with undimmed beauty. So the summer months passed—not one drop of rain, no harvest. The winter came, and still no moisture for the thirsty earth. I had no grain in store—it had been burned; no hay for my cattle—the grass had not grown. The cattle died, one after another, and through the long winter it was a fearful struggle to get bread to eat.

"Spring returned, and yet no rain. I had no grain to sow, and others began to be in want. We grew weak and sick at heart. We were in the midst of what this country had never known—a real famine. Terror took hold of the soul, while hunger tormented the body.

"Day and night we prayed for relief, and the answer, always the same, echoed and reechoed everywhere: 'Will a man rob God? Yet ye have robbed me. But ye say,

"Wherein have we robbed Thee?" In tithes and offerings. Ye are cursed with a curse; for ye have robbed me, even this whole nation.'

"Summer's burning heat poured down upon us, and one after another, my whole family sickened and died. Oh! The agony of watching over the sick beds with nothing to alleviate their suffering! To see our dearest friends dying of starvation! Yet so my loved ones died, and I lived on. I buried them with my own hands, for the famine had taken all sympathy from the community; each was fully occupied with his own sorrow.

"Day after day I wandered through the rooms of my desolate home and touched reverently the common things which their dear hands had used, and I found some comfort in this indulgence of my sorrow.

"But even this poor solace was taken away from me. Another fiery tempest came, sweeping away every remaining vestige of my earthly possessions, and I fled before it. On and on and on, still flying, still pursued, never tiring, impelled by a terror indescribable, till at length, I know not how, I found myself in a deep gorge of a California mine. All around me lay broken fragments of rich gold-laden quartz, the very earth beneath my feet seemed formed of golden sand, and on either side of the narrow valley the mountains rose, full of treasure. But all this wealth awakened no emotion, for yonder, trickling over the rocks, was water, pure cold water! Almost frantic with joy, I rushed toward it, but fell fainting ere my lips were moistened. I did not lose consciousness, but too weak with my utmost effort to drag myself onward, there I lay, with the lifegiving water almost within my reach!

"At last relief came; the miners gathered to the little grass plat not far away to eat their noonday meal. They seated themselves on the grass, made tables of the broken rocks, and spread out their bountiful repast. How delicious their food looked! I had not seen so much at one time for months. How I longed for the very crumbs that fell from their hands, yet I could not ask. It was not pride, but despair. All the ungrateful past of my life seemed to come up before me—the food I had carelessly wasted, or carelessly received, unmindful of the Giver. I never was hungry till this famine began, and now it seemed impossible for me ever to be fed. 'Cursed with a curse' for my ingratitude and robbery of God! Oh, the thought was agony! A deep groan escaped my lips and discovered me to the miners. One brought me a cup of water, and others gave me food. What a luxury was that cold water! How delicious was that coarse but wholesome food! I ate and drank like the famished creature that I was, till fully satisfied, and my kind friends returned to finish their own repast, leaving me lying on the soft grass with a heart full of praise and thanksgiving.

"The miners were rough men, of many nationalities. Irish, Germans, Chinese, and profane God-defying Americans, worked side by side. And as they sat in groups, enjoying their noonday meal, I listened to their fearful profanity till my soul was sick within me. There I lay, all that long summer afternoon, living over the years of my past prosperous life, bemoaning my selfishness and thinking how little I had ever done to send the gospel to such as the men in the mines.

"But all the future was dead within me. What could a poor, bereaved, famine-stricken man do, only to pray for pardon and for death?

"At last the day was ended, and two of the kind miners, half led, half carried me to their camp, and shared their evening meal and their scanty tent with me. My heart was full of gratitude, and, before seeking repose, I knelt to thank Him who had given such unexpected deliverance from the famine and death.

"Scarcely had I lain down, when one of the men touched me on the shoulder saying, 'Stranger, if you can pray won't you come and see a sick man just over here?'

"I arose and followed him, and there in a dirty tent, lay, and had lain for weeks, tossing with fever and delirium, my once happy, innocent boy—my long lost Henry. The fever had left him, and now, pale and exhausted, he seemed only waiting for the last heartthrob of a wasted life. Some of you, my friends, have known of this great sorrow which has lain on my heart for years, and may imagine the meeting and the sad recital I had to make. He said little of himself till I asked him of his spiritual state—his preparation for an exchange of worlds. An expression of anguish passed over his face. 'I am not ready—not prepared,' he exclaimed. 'All is lost, lost! Don't interrupt me,' he continued, as I was about to speak. 'I know what you would say; I know the way but have lost desire to walk therein. I feel I am forever lost! Two years ago,' he continued, 'there came to the mines a young Christian minister, full of life and enthusiasm, yet so gentle and blameless, so Christlike that we must all love him. He had a wonderful power over all, even the roughest, and I loved him as a brother. He remained with us a year, preaching, talking, and praying, till profanity was banished, and many seemed almost persuaded. His second year's labors were scarcely begun when news came from the Home Missionary Society saying the treasury was empty, and they did not know how long it would be before they would be able to pay what remained due on his salary. And there were so many feeble churches needing a little help, so many new settlements to be occupied, that they could not continue his commission another year. His heart was full of grief. He loved those rough men. He would have gladly worked with his hands as did Paul, but had not the strength, nor could he live without the salary. The miners might have paid it, but they would not. They liked him, but he was a restraint upon them, and he left us. Father, I thought of home then, of those rich farms, those bountiful harvests, and those men and women professing so much love to Christ, yet neglecting to fully support their own minister and doing nothing to give these poor miners the Bread of Life. I might have been a Christian if young Hurd remained here, but when he went away I was angry with Christians, with God, and myself. I went back to my old ways, and now I cannot repent.' My poor boy sank back on his pillow, exhausted. A deadly pallor overspread his face, his breath grew shorter and shorter, and in my agony at seeing him dying thus without hope, I uttered a deep groan and awoke.

"At first I could scarcely believe it possible that what I had passed through was but a dream, and then such a flood of contending emotions poured in upon my soul as almost overpowered me. I was indeed like one rescued from the deepest misery and put in possession of every needful blessing. How happy I was, how grateful for the sparing mercy of my heavenly Father! And never did I receive any worldly good with half the satisfaction that it gave me to know that God would accept a thank offering at my hands. I was in haste to make the offering for I feared the old lifelong selfishness would come back to trouble me and I could see that my wife had the same fear.

"But the offering was made, gladly and in good faith, by us both. During the few days that have intervened since then, I have thoroughly investigated the subject of tithing, and it seems so reasonable, so just, indeed so very little to offer in return for our many mercies, that I only wonder why I, a professedly Christian man, could so long have been blind to my duty and privilege.

"Just think of it, year after year, I have plowed my fields and sowed the seed, utterly powerless to make one single seed germinate. I have planted orchards and could neither make the trees live nor the fruit grow. And every season, God has given the sunshine and the dew and the copious rain. And more wonderful still, he has constantly carried on that chemical process by which each plant has appropriated to itself the elements it needed for growth and perfection. Then, when the rich harvests have been gathered in, I have not brought to God a thank-offering of even one-twentieth of the fruits of the earth; and the little which I have doled out, I have called *benevolence*.

"And all these years, men, like the miners in my dream, men from the corrupt nations of the old world, whom God has sent to us for light, and our own people, somebody's sons, every one of them, have been going down to eternal death uninstructed and unwarned. While I, Cain-like, have said in my heart, 'Am I my brother's keeper?' O my brethren! God would be entirely just if He were to visit upon me all the horrors of that fearful dream.

"Yet he is long-suffering and abundant in mercy, and His fearful denunciation is followed by the comforting words: 'Bring ye all the tithes into the storehouse, that there may be meat in mine house, and prove me now herewith,' saith the Lord of Hosts, 'if I will not open you the windows of heaven, and pour you out a blessing that there shall not be room enough to receive it!'

"I cannot recall the past; I can only pray God to forgive it. But most gladly for the future, do I, from the depths of a grateful heart, adopt Jacob's vow: 'Of all that Thou shalt give me, I will surely give the tenth unto Thee.'"

A solemn hush pervaded that large assembly when Mr. Penniman ceased speaking, broken, at length, by Mr. Goodman's voice in prayer. A hymn was then sung and the meeting closed.

The Way of Escape

My heart ached for the wretched man. His debauch was over; his nerves unstrung; the normal sensibilities of a moral nature quickened after a brief torpor, into most acute perceptions. Such a haggard face! Such hopeless eyes! I see the picture now as a haunting spectre.

"Let the memory of this hour, so burdened by pain and repentance, be as a wall of defense around you in all the future," I said.

He looked at me drearily. Slowly shaking his head, he replied, "Such memories are no defense. My soul is full of them. When temptation assails, they fall away, and I am at the mercy of mine enemy, who rushes in, like a hungry wolf, to kill and to destroy."

"Is there no help for you, then?" I asked.

He shut his eyes and was very still. If an artist could have seen his face then and faithfully caught its expression, those who looked upon the image must have felt such pity in their hearts as makes the eyes grow dim with tears.

"I fear not," he answered, after a little while, in a hopeless kind of way.

"It cannot be." I spoke confidently and assuringly. "No man is given over to such utter ruin. There must be, and there is, a way of escape from every evil."

"Except evil of a bad   and degrading habit—that vile second nature," he answered, "the steady current of which is forever bearing him downward, downward, toward a storm-wrecked ocean. He may seize the oars in alarm, as I have done scores of times, and pull against the current, making head for a little while. But, human strength avails not here. The arms grow weary; the spirit flags—it is easier to drift than to row and down the current bears him again. It is the history of thousands and tens of thousands, and I am no exception."

"It cannot be," I answered. "There is help for every man, no matter how weak, nor how beset by enemies, else God's word must fail."

"It does fail, I think," he answered, in a gloomy, despairing kind of way.

"No! No! No!" Quickly and emphatically did I reject his conclusion.

"Have it as you will. I shall not argue the point." He spoke almost listlessly.

"Then, I say there is help for every man, no matter where he is or what he is. We cannot fall so low that the Everlasting arms are not still beneath us, ready to bear us upward to mountain heights of safety."

"Oh, that those arms would bear me upward!" almost groaned my poor friend. "I have no strength in myself. I cannot climb. Unless lifted by another, I must perish."

"So bad as that?" I said.

"Just so bad," he answered, slowly and bitterly. "This second nature I have made for myself, is my ruler. Reason, conscience, the love of my wife and children, my good reputation, pride, manliness—all human powers and virtues are its slave. And such a bondage!"

There was not a ray of hope in his dreary eyes.

"You must try again," I said, cheerily. "No man need be a slave."

"Easily said!" was his impatient answer, "while yet all men are slaves to some habit from which they cannot break."

"Say, rather, from which they will not break."

"You mock me with idle words."

"No; I speak only the words of truth and soberness. There is human strength, and there is divine strength. The Everlasting arms are always beneath and ready to bear us up, if we will but lean upon and trust them. Human strength is but as a broken reed; divine strength is sure as God Himself. It never fails."

There came into his heavy eyes a feeble play of light. The stern rejection that sat upon his lips faded off.

"In our own strength, nothing," I said, "in God's strength, all."

I saw his hands moving in an uncertain way. Then they rested one against the other. Suddenly they were clasped together in a kind of spasm, while his eyes flashed upward in a wild, half-despairing appeal to God, his lips groaning out the words, "Save me, or I am lost!"

Even now, memory gives back the thrill that swept along my nerves as his cry penetrated my ears.

Never from any human soul went up, unheard, a prayer like that. He who once and forever took upon Himself our nature, and who was in all points tempted as we are yet without sin, and who is touched always with the feeling of our infirmity, stands close beside us, knocking at the door of our heart that He may come in and help and save us. All hell is powerless before Him. Impure desires flee from His presence like night birds when the sun rises, and the cords of evil habits are broken, as the withes that bound the arms of Samson, at His lightest touch.

I waited for a while without speaking watching him closely, to see if he would rise into anything like confidence. Gradually, the hard, desponding look faded from his countenance, and I saw a calm resolve begin to show itself about his mouth.

"One effort more," he said, at last, speaking slowly, but very firmly, "One effort more, but not in my own strength. I have tried too often, and shall never try it again. I give up the struggle as hopeless. If God fails me, I am lost."

What a fearful crisis! If God fail? He never fails—is never nearer to us, nor stronger to help us, than at the moment when, despairing of our own strength, we turn to Him. The only danger lies in our not trusting Him fully.

"But how shall I trust Him? How shall I get a transfer of His strength to my will? How is it that this power can supplement my weakness? I am away down in the valley of sin and shame; how am I to get upon the mountains of purity, peace and safety? Will He bear me up as on the wings of an eagle? Or must I climb and climb, from day to day, until I reach the summit?"

"You must climb," I said.

"I cannot. I have no strength. I have tried it a hundred times and failed." He answered with the returning doubt.

"And you will fail again if you trust in your own strength. But with God-given strength, used as your own, the ascent is sure."

"Ah! I see!" Light broke all over his face. "I see! I see!" he repeated. "God does not lift us out of our sins and misery, but gives us divine strength, if we ask Him in all sincerity, by which we lift ourselves."

"Yes."

"It is very simple and clear." He drew a long breath of relief, like one who has a load taken from his mind.

"The law of our dependence on God for help," I said.

"Yes. And now I see the meaning of this sentiment, in an old hymn I often heard sung when I was a boy, and which always struck me as a paradox: "'When I am weak, then am I strong.'"

"The Christian poet," I answered, "lifted into something of inspiration, often sees truth in clearer light than we do who are down among the mists and shadows."

"Ah me!" he sighed, "your closing words remind me of the depth at which I lie, and the almost infinite distances above me to which I must rise ere out of danger."

"And to which you may surely rise if you will," I answered with cheerful assurance.

"By God-given strength only!" he spoke, solemnly.

"Aye; never, never for an instant lose sight of that! Never, no matter how strong you may feel that you have grown, trust in yourself. In the hour of temptation, look upward, praying in the silence of your heart, for strength to resist."

"Best of friends!" he exclaimed, in deep emotion; "you must have been sent to me by God. Hope dawns on a night that has been starless. I see the way to safety—for me the only way. No one knows but myself how hard I have tried to reform, nor in how many ways I have sought to escape from a terrible thralldom. But all has been in vain. When this remorseless appetite that has enslaved me, asserted itself my will became as nothing."

Long time we talked, I saying all that I could to strengthen him.

On the next Sabbath, much to my surprise and pleasure, I saw him at church with his wife. I could not remember when I had seen him there before. At the close of the services, as I moved down the aisle with the crowd, someone grasped my hand and gave it a strong pressure. I turned and looked into the face of the friend I had tried to save.

"Oh, Martin!" I said, as I received a glance full of meaning and then his hand pressure.

We walked for a few moments side by side without speaking and then were separated by the crowd.

On the Sabbath following, he was at church again; and Sabbath after Sabbath found him in the family pew, that for years had seen him so rarely.

Three or four months went by, and Martin's feet were still in the paths that led upwards. But one day I was shocked to hear that he had fallen again. On careful inquiry, I learned that he had been with his wife to an evening entertainment given by a citizen of high worth and standing, whose name is on every lip as munificent in charity; but who, whatever may be his personal conviction, is not brave enough to banish wine from the generous board to which he invites his friends. And I learned still farther, to my grief and pain, that the glass which broke down the good resolution of Martin, and let in upon him the fierce flood of repressed appetite, was proffered by the hand of this good citizen, as host.

I lost no time in going to my poor friend. I found him way down the valley of humiliation, his soul in the gall of bitterness. Shame and sorrow were in his heavy eyes, but not despair. I took hopeful notice of this.

"It is very hard for us, all but God forsaken wretches!" he said bitterly, after the first formal sentence had passed between us. "Mr.— is a man of generous feeling. He gives, in a princely way, to churches and to charities; he is one of our best and most liberal citizens; and yet, after I have taken a few steps heavenward, he puts a stumbling block in my way and I fall back toward hell!"

"You could not have fallen over any stumbling block man or devil might place in your way," I answered, "if you had been walking in divine, instead of human strength."

"Well do I know that," he replied.

"And so," I said, "let this sad fall keep you in a more vivid remembrance of human weakness. Never for one instant trust in yourself. Stand perpetually on guard. The price of your liberty is eternal vigilance."

"It is a hard fight," he said, with a sigh, despondingly.

"Life is a warfare," I replied. "We are all beset with enemies who know too well our vulnerable places— enemies that never sleep—implacable, cruel, ever seeking our destruction. I, you, all men have them. Trusting only in human strength, no one gains a victory; but in divine strength the issue of battle is sure. And so, my friend, gird up your loins again and be wary and valiant."

Hope and courage came back into his heart.

"Beware of ambush," I said, as I parted from him that day. "The enemy, coming on you unawares, is more to be dreaded than when he forms his line of attack to the sound of trumpets. Seek no conflicts; keep off his ground; but when he comes forth to meet you, giving challenge, do battle in the name of the Lord."

A few weeks afterward I was present when a gentleman of large wealth and good standing, both in church and society, said to him, "I didn't see you at my house last evening."

"No," was the rather curt reply; "it is safer for me to keep off the devil's ground."

"I don't understand you, sir!" replied the gentleman, a flush of sudden anger in his eyes, for he felt the remark as a covert insult.

Martin's face grew sober, and he answered with a calm impressiveness that caused the anger to go out of his listener's eyes, and a thoughtful concern to take its place.

"I am fighting the devil," he said, "and must not give him the smallest advantage. Just now I am the victor and hold him at bay. He has his masked batteries, his enchanted grounds, his mines and pitfalls, his gins and miry sloughs; and I am learning to know the signs of hidden danger. If I fall into any of his snares, I am in peril of destruction; and though I struggle or fight my way out, I am weak or wounded, and so the less able to meet the shock of battle when he rushes upon me as I stand on guard ready in God's name, for the conflict.

"His enchanted ground is a social company, where wine flows freely. I speak of what it is to me, and call it, so far as I am concerned, the devil's ground. He caught me there not long ago and had me at his own advantage. But I will not again set foot thereon. If you, good citizens, make of your homes, in mistaken hospitality, places where the young find temptation, and the weak, stumbling blocks, such men as I am must shun them as they would the gates of hell."

His manner had grown more and more impressive.

"Is it so bad as that?" remarked the gentleman, in a voice that showed both surprise and pain.

"Just so bad," Martin answered impressively; "I believe Reigart's oldest son was at your house?"

"Yes."

"It was the devil's ground for him. An hour or two ago I saw him coming out of a saloon, so drunk that he could not walk straight. And only three days ago, his father told a friend that his boy had certainly reformed and that he now had more confidence in his future than he had felt for a long time."

"You cannot mean what you say?" The gentleman exclaimed in visible agitation.

"I have told you only the sad and solemn truth," was Martin's answer; "and if I had accepted your invitation, I might now be lying at a depth of misery and degradation— the bare thought of which makes me shudder!"

The gentleman stood for a little while as if stunned.

"This is frightful to think of," he said, and I saw him shiver. "It is the last time," he added, after a pause— "the last time that any man shall go out of my house weaker and more degraded than when he came in. If my offering of wine causes my brother to offend, then will I not offer it again while the world stands."

"Ah, sir!" answered Martin, "if many, many more of our good citizens would so resolve, hundreds of young men now drifting out into the current of intemperance might be drawn back into safer waters; and hundreds of others who are striving to make head against it, saved from destruction. I speak feelingly, for I am one of those who is struggling for life in this fatal current."

The way of safety for a man like Martin is very narrow and straight. If he steps aside into any of the pleasant paths that open on the right hand and on the left, he is in the midst of peril. If he grows confident on that which is given from above, the danger of falling becomes imminent.

Martin fell again. Alas! That this should have to be told.

"Was that Martin who passed us?" asked a friend with whom I was walking.

"No," I answered in a positive voice. Yet, as I said the word my heart gave a throb of fear—the man was so like him.

"It was; I am sure. Poor wretch! He tried hard to reform; but that cursed appetite is too much for him. I'm afraid there is no help. He'll die a drunkard."

I turned back; quickly and without a response, I followed the man we had passed. Just as I came up to him, he had stopped at the door of a drinking saloon and was holding a brief parley with awakened appetite.

"In God's name, no!" I said, lying my hand upon him.

He started in a frightened kind of way, turning on me a haggard face and blood shot eye. I drew my arm within his and led him away, passive as a child. Not a word was spoken by either, until we were in his office, which was not far distant, and the door shut and locked. He dropped into a chair, with a slight groan, his head sinking upon his chest. He was the picture of abject wretchedness.

"He leaveth the ninety and nine that are safely folded," I said, speaking in a low, tender voice, "and goeth out into the wilderness to seek that which is astray."

He did not answer.

"You have looked to the strong for strength, you have prayed to Him for succor, and He has come very near to you and helped you. Because you again went out of the fold, His love has not failed. He has found you out in the wilderness and brought you back to a place of safety. Only trust in Him, and all will be well. He is the friend that sticketh closer than a brother. His is a love that never fails."

I waited for him to reply, but he kept silence.

"It must have been no ordinary temptation," I said. Still he was silent.

"The enemy must have come on you unaware," I added, after a brief pause. "The bolt must have fallen ere you saw the warning flash."

"I was taken at a disadvantage, but I had time to know my enemy and should have given the battle in God's name, instead of yielding like a craven."

Such was his reply. It gave me hope.

"Tell me the whole story," I said.

He raised himself to a firmer attitude, and I saw swift light beginning to flash in his dull eyes.

"Wounded again in the house of a friend," he replied.

"What friend?"

"One on whom God has laid the special duty of saving souls—our minister!"

"Not Mr. L?"

"Yes."

I was confounded.

"I went to him for help," continued Martin, "and instead of the counsel and support I then so much needed, for my old enemy, appetite, was gathering up his strength, and setting his host in battle array, I was tempted and betrayed! I should have gone to God and not to man. With His divine word in my thought and prayer in my heart, I should have opposed the awakening enticement of desire, as I have so often done and prevailed."

"Tell me how it happened," I said.

"As I have just told you," he replied, "I was not feeling very strong. That old restlessness of which I have spoken, had come back upon me, and I knew what it meant. So I said to my wife, 'I think, Mary, that I'll step around and see Mr. L. I'd like to talk with him.' She looked at me with a slight shadow of concern in her face, for she has learned to know the signs of a coming hour of darkness when the powers of hell renew their direful assaults upon my soul. 'Do,' she answered, and I went.

"I found Mr. L. in his library but not alone. Mr. E., the banker, had called to talk with the minister about a college for theological students, in which both felt considerable interest. Funds were wanted in order to give the institution the required efficiency, and the ways and means of getting the funds were earnestly discussed by Mr. L. and the capitalist. After an hour's talk, and the arrangement of a plan for securing the object in view, Mr. L. rang a bell. To the servant who came in, he said something in a low voice, that I did not hear. The servant retired, but came back in a few minutes, bearing, to my surprise and momentary consternation, a tray with wine and glasses. I saw a pleased look in the banker's eyes as they rested upon the amber-colored wine.

"'Some fine, old sherry,' said Mr. L., 'sent me by a friend abroad. I want you to taste it.' And he filled the three glasses that were on the tray, handing one to his guest and another to me. In myself—my poor, weak self—I was not strong enough to refuse. If I had looked up to God, instantly, and prayed for strength to do the right, strength would, I know, have come. But I did not. I took the glass, not meaning to drink, but to gain time for thought. To have refused, would have been, I then felt, to set myself up as a rebuker of these men; and that I had not the courage to do. No, I did not mean to taste the wine. But, as they lifted their glasses, drank, and praised the fruity juice, I, in a kind of mesmeric lapse of rational self-control, raised my glass also, and sipped. A wild, fierce thirst possessed me instantly, and I drained the glass to the bottom.

"A sudden terror and great darkness fell upon me. I saw the awful gulf on whose brink I stood. 'I will go home,' I said to myself, and rising, I bade the two men an abrupt good-night and left them. But I did not go directly home, alas for me! There are too many enticements by the way. Indeed, I don't know how or when I got home.

"Of the shame, the anguish, the despair of this morning, I cannot speak. You don't know what it means— to have no plummet by which to sound its depths of bitterness. I left home for my office, feebly resolved to keep away from temptation—how feebly, you know! If the good Lord who is trying to save me, had not sent you to my rescue, I would now be—oh! I cannot speak the frightful words."

"He never leaves us nor forsakes us," I answered. "He is always going out upon the bleak mountains, to the hot desert, and into the wilderness of wild beasts, seeking His lost and wandering sheep. If they hear His voice and follow Him, He will bring them into his fold, where is peace and safety."

"Good Shepherd of souls." My friend said, audibly, lifting upwards his eyes that were full of tears, "save me from the wolves! They wait for me in all my paths; they spring upon me in all my unguarded moments; they hide themselves in covert places, thirsting for my life; they steal upon me in sheep's clothing—they beset me everywhere! Good Shepherd! I have no help but in Thee."

Breaking the deep, impressive silence that followed, I said, "In Him alone is safety. So long as you hear His voice and follow Him, no wolf can touch you with his murderous teeth. But, I you go out of His sheepfold and trust in your own strength to overcome the wild beasts that crowd the wilderness of this world, destruction is sure."

A few years have passed since then, and Martin still holds, in divine strength, the mastery of appetite. The vile second nature he had formed unto himself, and which bore him downward for a time in its steady current, grew weaker and weaker, as the new life, born from above, gained strength. In the degree that he resisted and denied the old desires, did they grow weaker; and in their place, God gave him purer and healthier desires, so that he became, as it were, a new man.

"The wolves are not all dead," I said to him one day, as we talked of the present and past.

He looked a little sober as he replied, "No, my friend. I often hear them howling in the distance; and I know full well that if I leave my Shepherd's side and stray off into the wilderness, vainly trusting myself, that I shall be as powerless to stand against them as a helpless sheep. For me, I am not safe for a moment, except when I trust in God's strength to supplement my weakness. When I do that, all hell cannot prevail against me!"

Caution

Was there a bright and glorious summer sky
    Ever so pure and clear,
But black and rugged clouds were hovering nigh,
    To make it dull and drear?
Was there an Eden e'er so blithe and gay,
    And free from jealous care,
But busy change, some dark, unwelcome day,
    Brought grief and sorrow there?

When, blessed with pleasant days, and fortune's
       smile,
    Our life untroubled grows,
'Tis best to guard in watchfulness, the while,
    Against unlooked for foes;
And while we thank the Lord for mercies past,
    And blessings day by day,
'Tis best ahead a watchful eye cast,
    And watch as well as pray.

A Quarrelsome Neighbor

"That man will be the death of me yet," said Paul Levering. He looked worried but not angry.

"Thee means Dick Hardy?"

"Yes."

"What has he been doing to thee now?" asked the questioner, a friend, named Isaac Martin, a neighbor.

"He's always doing something, friend Martin. Scarcely a day passes that I don't have complaint of him. Yesterday one of the boys came and told me he saw him throw a stone at my new Durham cow and strike her on the head."

"That's very bad, friend Levering. Does thee know why he did this? Was thy Durham trespassing on his grounds?"

"No, she was only looking over the fence. He has spite against me and mine and does all he can to injure me. You know the fine Bartlett pear that stands in the corner of my lot adjoining his property?"

"Yes."

"Two large limbs full of fruit hung over on his side. You would hardly believe it, but it is true, I was out there just now and discovered that he had sawed off those two fine limbs that hung on his side. They lay down upon the ground, and his pigs were eating the fruit."

"Why is Dick so spiteful to thee, friend Levering? He doesn't annoy me. What has thee done to him?"

"Nothing of any consequence."

"Thee must have done something. Try and remember."

"I know what first put him out; I kicked an ugly old dog of his once. The beast, half starved at home, I suppose, was all the time prowling about here and snatched up everything that came in his way. One day I came upon him suddenly and gave him a tremendous kick that sent him howling through the gate. Unfortunately, as it turned out, the dog's master happened to be passing along the road. The way he swore at me was dreadful. I never saw a more vindictive face. The next morning a splendid Newfoundland, that I had raised from a pup, met me shivering at the door, with his tail cut off. I don't know when I have felt so bad. Poor fellow! His piteous looks haunt me now; I had no proof against Dick but have never doubted as to his agency in the matter. In my grief and indignation I shot the dog and so put him out of sight."

"Thee was hasty in that, friend Levering," said the Quaker.

"Perhaps I was, though I have never regretted the act. I met Dick a few days afterwards. The grin of satisfaction on his face I accepted as an acknowledgment of his mean and cruel revenge. Within a week from that time one of my cows had a horn knocked off."

"What did thee do?"

"I went to Dick Hardy and gave him a piece of my mind."

"That is, thee scolded and called him hard names and threatened."

"Yes, just so, friend Martin."

"Did any good come of it?"

"About as much good as though I had whistled to the wind."

"How has it been since?"

"No changes for the better; it grows, if anything, worse and worse. Dick never gets weary of annoying me."

"Has thee ever tried the law with him, friend Levering? The law should protect thee."

"Oh, yes, I've tried the law. Once he ran his heavy wagon against my carriage purposely and upset me in the road. I made a narrow escape with my life. The carriage was so badly broken that it cost me fifty dollars for repairs. A neighbor saw the whole thing and said it was plainly intended by Dick. So I sent him the carriage-maker's bill, at which he got into a towering passion. Then I threatened him with a prosecution, and he laughed in my face malignantly. I felt the time had come to act decisively, and I sued him, relying on the evidence of my neighbor. He was afraid of Dick and so worked his testimony that the jury saw only an accident instead of a purpose to injure. After that, Dick Hardy was worse than ever. He took an evil delight in annoying and injuring me. I am satisfied that in more than one instance he left gaps in his fences in order to entice my cattle into his fields that he might set his dogs on them and hurt them with stones. It is more than a child of mine dares to cross his premises. Only last week he tried to put his dog on my little Florence, who had strayed into one of his fields after buttercups. The dog was less cruel than the master or she would have been torn by his teeth, instead of being only frightened by his bark."

"It's a hard case, truly, friend Levering. Our neighbor Hardy seems possessed of an evil spirit."

"The spirit of the devil," was answered with feeling.

"He's thy enemy, assuredly, and if thee does not get rid of him he will do thee great harm. Thee must if thee would dwell in safety, friend Levering."

The Quaker's face was growing very serious. He spoke in a lowered voice and bent towards his neighbor in a confidential manner.

"Thee must put him out of the way."

"Friend Martin!" the surprise of Paul was unfeigned.

"Thee must kill him."

The countenance of Levering grew black with astonishment.

"Kill him!" he ejaculated.

"If thee doesn't kill him he'll certainly kill thee, one of these days, friend Levering. And thee knows what is said about self-preservation being the first law of nature."

"And get hung!"

"I don't think they'll hang thee," coolly returned the Quaker. "Thee can go over to his place and get him all alone by thyself, or thee can meet him on some byroad. Nobody need see thee, and when he's dead, I think people will be more glad than sorry."

"Do you think I'm no better than a murderer; I, Paul Levering, stain my hands with blood!"

"Who said anything about staining thy hands with blood?" asked the Quaker, mildly.

"Why, you!"

"Thee's mistaken; I never used the word blood."

"But you meant it. You suggested murder."

"No, friend Levering. I advised thee to kill thy enemy, lest some day he shall kill thee."

"Isn't killing murder, I should like to know?" demanded Levering.

"There are more ways than one to kill an enemy," said the Quaker. "I've killed a good many in my time, and no stain of blood can be found on my garments. *My way of killing enemies is to make them friends.* Kill neighbor Hardy with kindness, and thee'll have no more trouble with him."

A sudden light gleamed over Mr. Levering's face, as if a cloud had passed. "A new way to kill people."

"The surest way to kill enemies, as thee'll find, if thee'll only try."

"Let me see. How shall we go about it?" said Paul Levering, taken at once with the idea.

"If thee has the will, friend Levering, it will not be long before thee will find the way."

And so it proved. Not two hours afterward as Mr. Levering was driving into the village, he found Dick Hardy with a stalled cartload of stone. He was whipping his horse and swearing at him passionately, but to no purpose. The cart wheels were buried halfway to the axles in stiff mud and defied the strength of one horse to move them. On seeing Mr. Levering, Dick stopped pulling and swearing and getting on the cart, commenced pitching the stones off on the side of the road.

"Hold on a bit, friend Hardy," said Levering, in a pleasant voice, as he dismounted and unhitched his horse. But Dick pretended not to hear, and kept on pitching off the stones. "Hold on, I say, and don't give yourself all that trouble," added Mr. Levering, speaking in a louder voice, but in a kind of cheering tone. "Two horses are better than one. With Charlie's help we'll soon have the wheels on solid ground again."

Understanding now what was meant, Dick's hands fell almost nerveless by his side. "There," said Levering, as he put his horse in front of Dick's and made the traces fast. "One pull and the thing is done." Before Dick could get down from the cart it was out of the mud hole, and without saying a word more, Levering unfastened his horse from the front of Dick's animal and, hitching up again, he rode on.

On the next day, Mr. Levering saw Dick Hardy in the act of strengthening a bit of weak fence through which Levering's cattle had broken once or twice, thus removing temptation and saving the cattle from being beaten and set on by dogs.

"Thee's given him a bad wound, friend Levering," said the Quaker, on getting information of the two incidents mentioned, "and it will be thy own fault if thee does not kill him."

Not long afterwards, in the face of an approaching storm and while Dick Hardy was hurrying to get in some clover hay, his wagon broke down. Mr. Levering, who saw from one of his fields the accident and understood what its loss might occasion, hitched up his team, and sent his own wagon over to Dick's assistance. With a storm coming on that might last for days and ruin from two to three tons of hay, Dick could not decline the offer though it went against the grain to accept a favor from the man he had hated for years and injured so many ways.

On the following morning, Mr. Levering had a visit from Dick Hardy. It was raining fast. "I've come," said Dick, stammering and confused, and looking down on the ground instead of into Mr. Levering's face, "to pay you for the use of your team yesterday, in getting my hay. I should have lost it if you hadn't sent your wagon, and it is only right I should pay you for the use of it."

"I should be very sorry," answered Paul Levering, cheerfully, "if I couldn't do a neighborly turn without pay. You are quite welcome, friend Hardy, to the wagon. I am more than paid by knowing that you saved that nice field of clover. How much did you get?"

"About three tons. But Mr. Levering, I must—"

"Not a word if you don't want to offend me," interrupted Levering. "I trust there isn't a man around here that wouldn't do as much for a neighbor in time of need. Still, if you feel embarrassed—if you don't wish to stand my debtor, pay me in goodwill."

Dick Hardy raised his eyes slowly and, looking in a strange wondering way at Mr. Levering, said, "Shall we not be friends?" Mr. Levering reached out his hand. Hardy grasped it with a quick short grip, and then, as if to hide his feelings that were becoming too strong, dropped it and went off hastily.

"Thee's killed him!" said the Quaker, on his next meeting with Levering; "thy enemy is dead!"

"Slain by kindness," answered Paul Levering, "which you supplied."

"No, thee took it from God's armory where all men may equip themselves without charge and become invincible," replied the Quaker. "And I trust for thy peace and safety, thee will never use any other weapons in fighting with thy neighbors. They are sure to kill."

Discord

It had some grains of truth, at least,
　　That fable of the Sybarite,
For whom, because one leaf was creased,
　　The rose-strewn couch had no delight.
'Tis pity that one thwarting thought,
　　One adverse chance, one sudden fear
Or sharp regret can turn to naught
　　The full content that seemed so near!
But this strange life of ours abounds
　　With notes so subtile, they afford
A thousand discords and harsh sounds
　　For one harmonious, perfect chord.

A Change of Place

Alfred Rogers was a skillful young mechanic in the city of Hartford more than thirty years ago, but like many a young man of that day and this, he had fallen into evil habits. Not all the endearments of a loving home circle could win him from the enchantment of the occasional glass and when the first was taken another and another were sure to follow, until a week was very likely lost in a "drunken spree."

An old writer used to give us a very good reason for not drinking—that it consumed too much time. It took "one day of sinning, one of suffering and one of repenting," every time he indulged in his cups.

Alfred had an excellent friend in a lady who had received him into her family when a boy and had always taken the deepest interest in his welfare. Not long after his marriage she had interceded with a gentleman, who employed many workmen, to take him into his establishment, feeling that his welfare for time and eternity might depend upon that decision.

That man had many scruples, fearing the influence of one who was intemperate upon his young apprentices. But Alfred consented to sign the pledge to abstain from "ardent spirits," which, with the little light then existing was considered all that could be reasonably asked of a man. I do not fully understand the nice distinctions made about the kinds of liquors, but there seems to have been various sorts of intoxicating drinks that were not counted as "ardent spirits." These the young man felt his pledge did not require him to abstain from.

For a while all went smoothly. Alfred was valued as a superior workman. He was respected everywhere, and his family were handsomely supported. But in an evil day a glass of something not called "ardent spirits," set on fire the old smoldering embers of a depraved taste. A second and a third glass fanned the blaze until it fired every drop of blood in his veins. The result was, not "one day of sinning, another of sorrowing and another of repenting," but two whole weeks of drunken insanity. Knowing that his wife had some money, he gave her no peace by day or by night until she gave it up to him. Then he set out for New York, where he spent it all in wild carousals, pawning a part of his clothing, and coming home at last a miserable, despicable object. "Who hath woe?" Surely there can hardly be a woe more terrible on earth than that of the drunkard and his family.

But yet he was not wholly lost, for when he came to himself he was overwhelmed with despair and self-reproach. Days of repenting were long and many, yet he shunned the path which led to his old employers. How could he hope to be received again after all that had transpired. But he hears that the Spirit of the Great Master goes out after the lost sheep and seeks diligently for them among the dark mountains of sin; perchance he may save them from being dashed to pieces upon the fearful rocks.

"Why do you not come back to the shop, Alfred?" he asked kindly.

With a look of anguish and despair in his bloodshot eyes, he said, "I never can come into your shop again; I have abused your confidence, treated you with the basest ingratitude, and destroyed my last hope of reformation."

A few strong, earnest, cheering words were like oil on the troubled waters of his heart. He clutched like a drowning man at a straw to hope that he might be a man again. He came to the shop and worked more faithfully than ever to prove his gratitude to the hand so kindly held out to him in his time of need.

Three bright months and then a terrible fall again. Ah, what a tyrant is depraved appetite! It is stronger than a man's love of respectability or happiness of the wife and child—stronger than his fear of eternal retribution!

At every successive fall Alfred sunk deeper into the mire. This time he grew so violent that he was obliged to be put under arrest.

Another season of suffering and repenting and then another trial in the lesson of forgiving until "seventy times seven."

The intervals of sobriety also became shorter and shorter, and the days of drunken debauch longer and more terrible, as the tyrant got the young man more and more into his clutches.

At last one bright May morning he was gone, no one knew whither; his missing presence would seem to have been a relief in the home where he was so often a terror and a curse. But oh, who can measure the depths of a woman's love for even the most worthless son or husband. How the poor bruised heart goes out in all their wanderings, yearning over them and praying for them in all the years of neglect and unkindness.

So Mary Rogers watched and prayed for the return of her worthless husband. When at last in mid-summer a letter came, stating where he was and that he had got steady work and begging her to come to him, with many promises of reformation, the poor trusting heart believed them all, and taking her little child she went to him. There were enough to sneer at her faith in such promises, to call her a fool for trusting to them after her past experience, but she heeded them not.

Two years and a half rolled away when a respectable, well-dressed man walked into the door of the old workshop and advanced with a manly, ringing step to meet the proprietor. Could it be Alfred Rogers changed? All that haggard, downcast look was gone. The face had the glow of health and cheerfulness; the bearing, that of a steady and prosperous man.

You may be sure there was a warm grasp of the hand for him and a cordial greeting. In answer to his inquiries Alfred replied emphatically, "I am well, *well* in more senses than one. It is over two years since I have tasted a drop of anything that can intoxicate. That was the only thing for me; I began abstaining from ardent spirits alone—but that was not enough—I could not reform that way. Now I have shut down on everything that can intoxicate, and you see the result."

After various kinds of inquiries after the welfare of his family, to all which he would give most pleasing answers, Alfred went on to say, "I have come now to tell you why I left you. I saw clearly that I should die if I did not leave off drinking and that I never could leave off in Hartford. I could not turn a corner of the street without passing a grogshop. I could not go to my meals without meeting some associate who asked me to take a glass. The dealers themselves would use every art to entice me to drink, well knowing that I would not stop after the first glass until they had a good bill against me. My only hope was in going where liquor was not to be had."

He remained away from the city some five years, returned to his old business thoroughly reformed, and became an active, earnest worker in the church and Sabbath school.

He could pass the old haunts now with only a feeling of loathing and repulsion.

What was the secret of this man's reformation?

It was in entire abstinence from everything that would intoxicate, and to succeed in this he went where liquor was not to be had. Otherwise he would have soon laid down in a drunkard's grave.

The Blighted Life

It was at a boardinghouse in one of our large cities, where I was expecting to sojourn for some months, that I made the acquaintance of Henry Somers. The first time I went to the table, he attracted my attention by his loquacity. He talked more than anyone else; but though his conversation was fluent and animated, his countenance did not light up. Indeed he had not an expressive face, and what expression there was, was not cheerful. It was that of a man with whom things were not going happily; of one who had something on his heart—some disappointment, some sorrow, some anxiety, some heavy care. At first I thought the sweet, gentle, youthful woman who sat beside him was his wife, but in this I soon found that I was mistaken—their proximity at the table being merely accidental, and their acquaintance not of long-standing. He had never been married.

Judging from his appearance, I should say that Somers, at this time, was approaching forty years of age. His dress was always most scrupulously neat, and his light brown hair and full handsome beard in perfect order. His blue eyes, though lusterless and surrounded with a dark circle, were always in motion, as if indictive of an uneasy, restless soul. His cheeks were somewhat sunken, and his face pale.

As the season advanced, I became better acquainted with my fellow boarder and found that he had been quite a traveler having not only been in Europe, but in China and Japan. I discovered, too, that he belonged to a wealthy family and that he had enjoyed opportunities of improvement far beyond what fall to the lot of most young men. But still there was not the intelligence and culture which such advantages should have given him. His conversation was quite disconnected and, sometimes, almost silly. Occasionally he seemed much dejected, talking about the unfeeling and heartless, selfish world, and his own hard lot and even wished he were dead. He had no employment, but told me that not long before he had almost completed arrangements for going into business but that the party failed to keep their word.

Two or three months had elapsed after my first meeting with my somewhat mysterious acquaintance when he disappeared from his place at the table for some days, and no one knew what had become of him. He had told no one of his intended absence, and his trunk and clothes were still in his room. Various were the conjectures, as day after day passed without his return. The mystery was soon solved. Learning one morning that he had come back the night before and that he was sick in his room, I went to see him. The first glance told the tale. He had been in a debauch and was now in the prostrate condition consequent upon days of drunkenness. I sat down by his bedside, spoke kindly to him, let him know that I understood the state of the case, that I wished to be his friend, and to do all in my power to help him up from his fall. Sympathy and kind words quickly unlocked his burdened heart, and he told me his sorrowful story. He had fallen in with so-called friends, who enticed him to drink and having once tasted he could not stop; he had lain several days at a public house under the influence of liquor, and the debauch having run its course, he had now come back, "in soul and in body," as he expressed it, "the most wretched man alive." With nerves unstrung, stomach disordered, burning thirst, an aching head, and an aching heart, he was indeed a pitiable spectacle.

But notwithstanding the evident sufferings of this miserable man, it was a relief to him to have someone present and especially one to whom he could unburden his oppressed and troubled soul. He told me his whole story. "This is not the first time," said he, "no, not by hundreds, that I have been as you see me. This thing has been going on for years. Long ago I contracted the habit of drinking, and it has clung to me with a power that I can't shake off. I am the son of a rich man and that has been my ruin. I had plenty of money and abundant opportunities of indulgence, and but for that my life would have been a very different one. My social position and ample means gave me access to a club, when I was quite young.

"There I met a gay, jolly set, and we used to play cards and take drinks night after night, until a very late hour. In this way things went on from bad to worse, until sometime I took a dozen or more drinks in a night, and of course never went home sober. This sort of life soon brought its natural consequences. My family were mortified and distressed. At first they plead and remonstrated; then they grew harsh and reproached. I was making a brute of myself, disgracing them. Various means were resorted to, to reform me, and after a time I was taken to Europe to get me out of the way of bad companions; but this did not help the matter much. Afterwards they sent me off to China, in hopes that the long voyage and change of life would break up my wretched habits; but this did not avail.

"I remained two years in the East and soon made the acquaintance of Englishmen who were harder drinkers than my old companions, and the only wonder is that I lived to get back to my own country. Perhaps it would have been better if I had died there, but I was spared and came home, and for a while strove to do better. Indeed I reformed so far that my father put me into business, but the accursed drink soon got the better of me. No longer fit for business, I was once more set adrift, and with old companions to help me on to ruin.

"What I have gone through since then, God only knows. Some time ago I concluded that I would make a desperate effort to break the horrible bondage, and, as it was important to get away from old haunts and companions, I came to this city. I am allowed just money enough to pay necessary expense; but even that, with the exception of a few dollars a month, is not risked in my hands. I had been keeping sober until I fell into this bad company, and then, as you see, I was overcome and I fear this will continue to be the way. What is to be the end—how long this wretched sort of life is to continue—I don't know; but if I were only ready for a better world, what a relief it would be to die!"

The foregoing was not given in the continuous form in which I have narrated it; he was suffering too much for that—nor in the precise words; but this is the story. He looked and talked like one who, although conscious of his frightful bondage, was yet hopeless as to his power to escape. I told him that God could help him, that his grace was all-sufficient, and that if with a penitent, broken heart, he would cast himself at the feet of the sinner's Friend, he would find mercy and be made a thoroughly reformed man, and that this was the only help that would certainly avail.

"I wish I were a Christian," said he; "what a blessing it must be to be a Christian! I should think you must be the happiest man in the world, with a Christian's hope, and spending your life in trying to do good."

This was spoken in the tone and manner of one whose bitter experience afforded a somber background for setting off his ideal of a Christian. But though the words were sincere, they were evidently but the passing utterances of a restless, disturbed spirit.

After a few moments silence, be said, "I'm like the man in the Bible—Esau, wasn't it? —who sold his birthright for a mess of pottage. I sold mine for a glass of liquor."

"Well, there's one thing," said I, "that you ought to do, and which I suppose you can do—that is to get some employment. You know the proverb 'An idle mind is the devil's workshop'; and so long as you are unemployed, you will be more liable to fall into temptation."

"I know that very well," he replied, "but how can I get employment? My father won't trust me with money, for he thinks I would soon waste it; and nobody would take a man into a business, who, they would be sure to find out, had been dissipated. And to tell the truth, I am not fit for business; my miserable course of life has injured my mind. I can't fix attention on anything, and what I undertook to do wouldn't be done well. The fact is, there's no hope for me. Oh, if I was only prepared, what a relief it would be to die!"

The tone and manner in which this was said showed that it came from a thoroughly wretched heart. It was the wail of woe from one who had made shipwreck of himself.

After this interview I not infrequently conversed with this unhappy man. His course was still the same— sometimes for months conducting himself well and then falling into a debauch. But at his best moments there was about him an air of misery and hopelessness, which always excited my sympathy. He went to the West some years since, and not long ago I read a notice of his death. Poor fellow! From what I have been able to gather about his last years, they were of a piece of his previous life, and no light shone upon his closing scene.

I have narrated the foregoing as a striking illustration of the wreck which bad habits, contracted in youth, make of entire subsequent life. This man was not cut off in the morning of his days; he lived to middle age. Nor did he sink to utter degradation. He never lay in the gutter; he was not a common outcast; nor did he die literally a drunkard's death. For years he saw the evil of his course and would fain have changed it, but when he had made the attempt, he could neither form the social ties nor make the business connections so essential to his continuance in well-doing.

What he said of himself indeed was true; he really was fit for nothing. His enfeebled mind rendered him an uninteresting companion; he was incapable of continuance and intelligent application; and he was restless as the troubled sea. All this, combined with shattered nerves and an irresolute will, made him apparently as unavailable for all the practical purposes of manhood as any human being I ever saw. Oftentimes I used to think what could be done for him, or with him, but there seemed nowhere to begin, nothing to build upon. Had he become a Christian that would have furnished the needful objective point, but thoughts on that subject came and went through his mind like water through a sieve. And so powerless was his will that if he made a pledge of abstinence, he would not keep it.

Here, then, was the sad spectacle of a man hardly yet in the noon of his days—restless, miserable, exiled by his family, without one intimate virtuous friend, and for practical purposes good for nothing. It was one of the most sorrowful illustrations I have ever met with of a blighted life. At the outset of his career he had every advantage— social position, wealth, influential friends, everything—but by yielding to the tempter these were all sacrificed. In those days and nights cardplaying drinking and jollity, no doubt seemed very fine; that was the seed-sowing, but when I saw him, the harvest time had come. He sowed to the wind and was reaping the whirlwind.

As I used to listen to the moaning of his wretched heart and feel how powerless I was to help him in such a case, oh, how my inmost soul pitied him; and how unspeakable seemed the folly of those who, with such beacons before them, deliberately and persistently follow in their footsteps. "Surely in vain the net is spread in the sight of any bird." So spoke Solomon; but it does not seem to be so now. The net stands right in the view, with its victims struggling in its meshes, and yet how many with eyes wide open walk right into it.

Young man, beware of dissipated company! Touch not, taste not, the fatal wine cup. Avoid the first step in the road to ruin and then you will not take the second. Take warning from the bitter experience of Henry Somers, lest like him sowing the poison seeds in youth, like him you reap the blighted life.

Not Myself

If not myself, then, who was I?

Just so. Who was I? That's the question. Perhaps, friendly reader, if I take you into my confidence, you will help me to see the matter in a clearer light, for I am just now in much obscurity.

"I was not myself" at the time. My friends said so, and I said so. It was my—and their—only apology and excuse.

"Mr. Jones is prudent and clearheaded and never would have done it if he had been himself." Everyone assented to this, and I accepted the declaration as true.

But how came it that I was not myself?

Had I been to a "circle" or "seance"? No; for I have no fancy for the sound of footfalls on the boundaries of another world. My business for the present is with embodied and not with a vagrant crew of disembodied spirits. Was I suffering from temporary insanity? No one, so far as I know, ever hinted to such a thing.

Let me tell you the whole story. I think it will interest you.

I am, or was, a merchant. For many years my business, under prudent management, had grown steadily, until the house over which I presided was known as one of the most prominent in the city. There are two pivots in every mercantile business on which success or failure rests—buying and selling. If the buyer of an establishment thoroughly understands his role, and the salesman his, success, in ordinary circumstances, is almost sure; but if either be seriously at fault, ruin is quite as certain.

I was, and always had been, the buyer in our house. To this part of the business I gave careful and systematic attention, keeping myself posted in regard to stocks of leading goods in market and the prospect of advancing or receding rates. Today I would buy freely, when others hesitated, because I was better informed, or had, from long observations and experience, a kind of intuition as to the future prices; but tomorrow found me cautious on a different line of goods, and I touched them lightly while others bought heavily. The results nearly always proved my skill or prescience.

There was no guess work in all this. I was educated to it. When I went to auction, or examined the importer's samples, I knew to a fraction what the article offered for sale was worth on the market, whether stocks in first hands were large or small and how much it would be prudent to buy.

During a period of ten years, in which scarcely a day passed that I did not go to auction or visit the sample room or store of some manufacturer, commission merchant or importer, no serious mistake in buying was made. In consequence, we were never caught with a large stock of anything on a falling market, but often got single advantages when prices went up.

But something came over me about three years ago, and every now and then I would make a slight mistake that annoyed me exceedingly, for I had grown proud of my skill and reputation as a buyer.

The first time this occurred, the mistake was so palpable that I made no attempt to excuse it. The case of goods I bought fell six cents a yard on the very next day. Every clerk in the store knew there would be a fall, and so did I. And yet, when the case was put up, I bid it off in my usual confident tone—the error flashing on me when it was too late for repair.

"I don't understand this," I said to myself, greatly annoyed by the incident. "What could have possessed me? The blunder has no excuse."

And yet, strange to say, within a month I committed a worse blunder. Now, if I had fallen into habits of intemperance, the thing would have been plain. But this was not the case. I am temperate in all things, in eating as in drinking. I don't mean that I am what is called a teetotaler for I consider myself a rational being and so put myself under the government of reason and not bonds. I take a glass of wine, or ale, or brandy whenever I think I need it and expect to continue doing so until I find that it does me harm, which is not yet. I can stop whenever I please.

Well, as I was saying, within a month I committed a worse blunder; stocking our shelves with a line of goods that fell twenty percent, I was annoyed, bewildered, and confounded.

"What has come over me? Am I losing my senses?" So I talked to myself. "There isn't a buyer of six months' experience that wouldn't have known better."

I put as good a face on the matter as possible and resolved never to be "caught napping again." Naturally, I was sensitive about the mistakes committed, and the remotest allusion to them annoyed me.

One of my partners, whose faith in my judgment these lapses had disturbed, ventured now and then a word of caution, especially when I was going to some large sale. I was never able to repress my irritation at this, and we had sharp words now and then, in consequence.

A great sale of goods, in our line, had been advertised in New York; the invoices covering, in the aggregate, nearly a quarter of a million dollars.

"Buy cautiously," said the partner whose faith in my judgment had been impaired.

"Hadn't you better go yourself?" I answered testily.

He looked at me with troubled eyes but made no response.

I went over to New York in the evening train, in company with several merchants on the same errand with myself. They talked up the matter of stocks of goods, the effect this heavy sale would have on prices, and the probable future of the market. Opinions differed. Some held that prices would advance, and some said they would recede. I listened and said but little, as was my habit, but carefully weighed all the *pros* and *cons* and considered all the reasons urged on both sides.

When I reached New York, my mind was made up to buy with great caution. It was barely possible that one or two leading capitalists in the trade might purchase heavily on speculation and hold for an advance; in that case, other buyers would make a good thing of it. But if the large stock went into several hands, each taking pretty freely, some, more eager to sell than the rest, might press the market and cause a serious decline in prices.

I saw this clearly and resolved to purchase only to the extent of supplying our immediate wants. But during the evening this purpose was disturbed and a different view adopted.

"Come to my room," said a well-known merchant who had been with me in the cars. It was after supper. "Two or three friends are to drop in for a talk over a bottle of wine about tomorrow's sale."

I went with him to his room. In a short time two merchants from my own city and one resident in New York joined us. Wine and cigars were ordered, and we spent two to three hours together, drinking, smoking and talking about the sale. I have never been able recall the data and reasonings by which I passed to the conclusion that my role on the next day was to be that of a heavy, instead of a light, buyer, but when I went to bed that night, such was my fixed purpose. I lay awake for a long time, pleasing my fancy with golden results that were sure to come from tomorrow's business. I counted the profits of our houses tens of thousands of dollars. Thoughts ran riot over the gains I would not fail to secure.

In thinking back to this night, I have always felt that I was not my real self—that in some way the perception of reasoning of another mind was superinduced upon my own—that my experience, clear judgment and prudence were lost for a period, and that my mental powers were operated by some volition foreign to my own.

I was not myself. That is certain. I was not fully myself on the next morning. On rising, my head ached in a dull way, and my brain was slightly confused. It was not clear to me that I was to make the fortune of our house by bidding off at the coming sale to the amount of fifty or a hundred thousand dollars. The wet blanket of doubt chilled my night's enthusiasm.

But a glass of brandy and water, followed by coffee and breakfast, cleared my head, gave life to my pulse, and tension to my nerves. I met my friend of the evening before, and we spent an hour previous to the sale in talking up the business of the day; and then, after emptying a bottle or two of wine, repaired to the auction rooms, which we found crowded with merchants from all parts of the country.

I was in a state of confidence and exhilaration— never had a clearer head, so it seemed, nor saw my way more distinctly. Terms were announced, and the sale began. Bidding was cautious at first, and a few lots were struck down at figures so low that I remember feeling disturbed as well as surprised. But the impression faded in a moment. On the next lot, I bid at the figure last obtained. Someone advanced, and I went higher promptly. The goods were mine, with no one going above me.

"Do you take the whole lot—forty cases?" asked the auctioneer.

"The whole," I answered in a confident way that caused many to turn and look at me.

The sale went on, growing more spirited as it progressed; new bidders ventured in at every successive lot. I forgot everything but my purpose to buy heavily and make the fortune of our house. A single idea possessed me, and that was the certain great advance in the price of the goods now being sold. I was as sure of this as of my existence and felt a kind of contempt for the timid buyers, who, with the opportunity of a hundred cases, took only five or ten.

A two o'clock, I left the heated auction with flushed face and throbbing temples. As the fresh air struck upon me with its grateful coolness, I seemed to pass into a new world of thought and perception. I was myself again—my clearheaded self—poised amid my own business experience and convictions.

What a shiver ran down my heart as the fact that I had just bid over sixty thousand dollars on a single line of goods looked me darkly in the face.

"Impossible!" I exclaimed, standing still, and catching my breath, for I seemed for the instant, as if in a vacuum. "Impossible! That would be ruin!"

And it was ruin! On the day after the sale, the goods that I had bought for a rise, fell twenty percent, and steadily declined day after day until they were fifty percent below the figures I had paid.

Stunned and bewildered by the peril in which my blind recklessness had plunged our house, we failed to do the only wise thing, which was to sell at once, and accept the inevitable loss of twelve thousand dollars. But none of us had the courage to look that disaster fairly in the face.

"The market will surely rally," we said. But it did not rally. We struggled with our fate, resorting to all kinds of expedients to keep our ship afloat—plunging, buffeting, gasping amid the waves, until by the storm and darkness the goodly vessel was stranded.

We saved little from that wreck. My partners gathered what to them remained and started on a new business venture, leaving me out.

Yes, I was left out—out in the cold, where I have been shivering ever since.

I was not myself when I bid so blindly. That my partners said—that our business friends, who pitied us, said—and that I said emphatically.

But, if not myself, who was I? You see, reader, I am back to where I started. Ever since the memorable day when I went to that auction room and acted the blind, overconfident, reckless speculator, instead of the cool, experienced, cautious businessman that I am and was, I have puzzled my brain over this question. Can evil spirits, who love to do us harm, get, through some strange process unknown to us, a temporary possession of our mental machinery, and drive it to our hurt or ruin? I have thought so sometimes. What happened to me, I have seen happen to others at various times in my life. One of the shrewdest and most wary buyers I ever knew, lost, suddenly, as I did, on a single occasion, his clearness of judgment and involved his house in a heavy loss. "I don't know what came over me," he said when I asked him about it. "Somehow, I was not myself on that day." He looked puzzled and worried when he said this.

A thought comes flashing across the darkness of my mind as I write and startles me! Can it bring a solution? Let me ponder. My brain did not have its normal steadiness and coolness on that night at the hotel when we discussed the coming sale. Why! Was it the fatigue of riding in the cars? No! I was used to that and not fatigued. The supper? Of course not. The wine?

I have walked the floor since writing the last sentence, in much agitation, and now sit down in a calmer state and with a clearer brain. I am afraid it was the wine? My judgment was clear when I went, on the night before the sale, to the room of my business friend and clouded when I left it, and yet it seemed clear. That is strange. It was an erroneous judgment and false in the light of my own true intelligence, and yet it looked fair to me that night. Perception was inverted. How? Why? I was not my own self.

On the next morning, this false judgment was in a wavering state. The convictions of the night previous were not so clear. I had disturbed doubts and troublesome questionings. I was by no means so confident that an advance in the market was to follow this large sale. What dispersed these doubts? What restored my confidence? Was it the nerve quieting brandy before and the exhilarating wine after breakfast? Did they give back that abnormal state of the brain, the result of unnatural stimulus through which I became, as it were, another, and not myself—acting the part of a blind and foolish speculator instead of the wise and prudent merchant that in my real self I was?

How is it? I am startled and shocked at such a view of the case. Strange, that this old saying should just now intrude itself—"When the wine is in, the wit is out!" There is no gainsaying that. And I, too, am out—out in the cold and all for what? A glass or two of brandy and a bottle of wine?